Leaves of the World Tree

A collection of short stories

By Adam Misner

To,

Leah

Table of Contents

Olaff   1

3 A.M.   15

The Smell of Pirates   22

SoulMates   59

Amorphous   67

There Are No White Knights   91

Olaff

Like many Olafs before him, he was named Olaff. It was not a bad name by any means. He shared his name with four others born that year, and he would share it with seven the year after. Olaf was then, as it had been before, and would be for generations to come, a common name. It was as though his parents had expected him to be average. Growing up he never felt as though he were different from the other boys. He was not scrawny and smart, or muscular and dumb, nor better or worse at most things. He threw the axe at the tree and hit five times out of ten, and his spear landed smack in the middle of everyone else's. It was only when they taught him how to write his name that he realized he was unique. His mother, being the literate one, had spelled his name with an extra "f."

Not every day was spent sprinting into battle. Like most of his days, he spent one in particular rowing. He sat on a long bench in the center of a large group of benches that were nearly identical and only distinguishable by their varying degrees of mold. As could be expected, if anything at all could be expected of such a regular person, he sat in the middle. Smack in the middle of everyone else, on his bench, between Vjolf and Bjorvak.

Vjolf and Bjorvak were both very unique warriors, not at

all like Olaff. Vjolf was not like other Nordlings. He was small and quick. Although he was half as large as your average Olaf he was twice as vicious. Instead of the traditional sword and shield or axe and shield combination, Vjolf held a curved sword he had looted from a boat filled with people who had been left out in the sun so long their skin had turned brown like an old dock. In his down time Vjolf took to hacking up the back of the sword until the nicks and chips made it look like a wood saw. In addition the little man carried around a sickle bound to a snapped spear haft. Why waste a good left hand when it can help you yank away shields and rip peasant throats?

Vjolf was good friends with his polar opposite and equally distinct friend, Bjorvak. He was not small like Vjolf nor as vicious in battle, but he was just as deadly. He was so large he rattled the bench with his gale blasting laughter every time Vjolf made a joke. In battle he was terrifying of an even greater caliber. His shield had the spear heads of every enemy javelin he had ever caught – or so he claimed – fastened to it. Olaff had seen him catch a lot of spears, sure, but not enough to cover his shield as completely as he had. They also tended to fall off, occasionally, when he bashed with his shield. The largest warrior on Hjalmmar Black-mane's ship could only possibly find one weapon heavy enough to match his massive muscles. And that was not a weapon in the slightest. At least not when it wasn't in Bjorvak's hands. The giant wielded an anvil wrapped in chains as a flail in battle. Rowing, by contrast, was more of something that kept his hands busy than any sort of physical chore.

And so Olaff with his extra "f" sat there next to a colossus of flesh, and far from being extraordinary. It was an ordinary day. One of the many days Olaff felt at home. The sky was gray and bland, and the ocean reflected the boredom right back. There were no birds to look at, not that there were none there. The birds simply were nothing to look at. There was no great hawk circling above, no omens of battle like a vulture. He couldn't even keep his back straight for the ravens of Odin, so they would give a good report back to the god of honorable death. All the sky was conquered by seagulls. Gray ones. Just like the sky and the ocean in blandness, but two fold in emptiness.

Olaff, like he had done many a time before, had begun staring cross-eyed at his beard. He was blonde like most northerners. But he was *so* blonde, so very Nordic, that his beard looked almost gray. Of course on Olaff's face the hair *was* gray. His personality and the light through the clouds conspired against his youth to make it so. To lessen the weight of the boredom inherent to rowing, he did what little he could while seated with his arms occupied by helping to propel a large creaky wooden vessel through the water. He had finished listening to the creaks of the wood imagining a conversation made of two words between two stains on the deck at his feet that resembled faces. Now he sucked in a breath, and exhaled through his nose.

His first breath was just like any other when he had resigned to this part of the cycle through his muses. He was hoping he could make even more of his tangled frizzy beard move with his next puff, and so he took in a deep breath. With his exhale he was surprised by something out of the ordinary. Unlike his previous exhales this time something touched his beard aside from air. Blood.

Olaff had not been punched in the face, so he knew it was not his. He uncrossed his eyes to see the source. The rower who sat in front of him, with the shiny helmet, was currently missing his enthralling head-wear. In its place was a newly formed fountain.

Olaff was not fast for a warrior but he was faster than the crossbow bolt that whizzed over his head as he ducked to get his sword.

*It's in my **pack**...* He thought.

He knew he couldn't get anything from that leather tomb he called a bag, not with his clumsy fingers. Amidst the battle cries from his companions and the shrieks of blades waking from their scabbards he swung under the bench to use both hands on the damnable container. He tore the flap open sending a bear tooth spinning across the deck. First he began worming his fingers behind his shield to reach his blade, but vertigo caught him once he saw where the shiny helmet had gone. He started tearing things out of his bag carelessly then resorted to dumping the entire bag out.

He grasped hold of his steel and was about to roll out from under the bench when Vjolf hit the deck in his path. He was covered in blood but there was none on his on his blades. Vjolf flailed but he was not going anywhere. He never would. Protruding from his neck was a trident. A weapon like a pitch fork with wide blades for prongs.

With Vjolf sprawled out gurgling blood in his way, Olaff had to crawl out over him awkwardly. Olaff went out on all fours, placing hands only where there was no blood that might slick his sword grip. He stood hastily, taking only enough time to make sure he was not standing on Vjolf. Olaff's head snapped left and right soaking in the scene. As he should have expected his foe to be, in the middle of the ocean, it was the merfolk. Seemingly harmless creatures to anyone who had never sailed with anything worth sinking. Mermaids, and mermen, had risen from the depths to try once again to take all they had. The mer-people did not bother to lure them to the deep with beautiful mermaids this time. They knew it would not work. He had neither the time nor the ability to count how many they faced, but it was enough. They were taller – or longer, rather – than he had realized. Even above the sides of the ship their lengthy tails let the merfolk tower over his fellow vikings.

My shield! He thought, with a pang of panic.

Olaff had left it under the bench in his mad rush to retrieve his weapon. He spun quickly on the blood slicked ground. Before he could think to retrieve his shield, however, he stopped. Slithering along the top of the bench was the long green tail of a merman. His first instinct won out over common sense and Olaff stabbed it, hard, pinning his sword through the bench.

The thing squealed, and whirled around furious. The merman's range of movement, however, was only as extensive as the sword stuck in the timber would allow. Olaff dove for the first weapon he could see. It was all the viking could do to avoid the creature's gleaming trident as it rushed toward his face. He had barely registered that he was holding Vjolf's sword before he had risen to face his opponent. He did not hesitate. He acted as though he had but a shard of a moment before the creature would attack. In reality, both he and his trident were pinned to the hard pine of the boat. The merman attempted to back-pedal away from the rushing blade, but rooted by the sword, he took the swipe across his throat all the same.

Olaff scanned the deck for comrades to assist as the algae colored blood spouted from his first – and most likely last – kill. He saw Bjorvak, almost immediately. He towered among a swarm of enemy fighters. The waterborn feared the anvil Bjorvak swung about his head, but they still surrounded him completely.

Olaff had heard stories that the people under the waves could turn into beasts. He thought little of those tales until he saw two of Bjorvak's foes change shape and grow. One borrowed aspects of a shark, while the other chose features of a crocodile. Before Olaff could make his way to Bjorvak, the oaf had lashed out at two or three mermaids at his right, exposing his front. The mer-shark used the opening to lunge over Bjorvak's shield and bite down hard on his chest.

Olaff stabbed deep into one of the merfolk surrounding Bjorvak and hacked at another. He fought hard, but he couldn't break through the ranks of Bjorvak's amphibious foes just yet. However, it did not seem the big man needed so much help from Olaff. Bjorvak dropped his shield and chain in favor of using both hands to pry the mer-shark from his chest. The shove was so sudden the shark-thing left teeth behind. It was so forceful that the body soared through the bulwark in an explosion of splinters and skipped along the surface of the water.

The whole event, from the heavy anvil hitting the deck to the chunk of bulwark being smashed into the sea, left the longboat rocking back and forth. Having only average sea legs in a situation such as this, usually means a fifty-fifty chance of becoming acquainted with the deck. Of course none of Olaff's opponents had any legs at all, let alone sea-legs, to keep them vertical.

Olaff looked up from the deck that had nearly felled him to see Bjorvak taking advantage of the tremor. The giant of a man was wildly raining down blows with an oar. The crocodile monster had no legs to stand on and the huge viking ensured he had no head either. Bjorvak was the strongest person Olaff had ever seen. It was nothing for him to turn that creature's head into paste. Being strong, however, had not made him observant. Unbeknownst to Bjorvak, his own chain had been wrapped around one of his muscular calves by a crawling mermaid with a spearhead wedged into her spine.

Olaff shouted incoherently at him but there was nothing he could say. No amount of yelling could teach Bjorvak how to swim. A stealthy mermaid pushed the anvil over the edge and the chain was taut in an instant. It was a quick journey on a slippery red and green road to the brink. Three or four quick thrusts of a trident later, and the man's gargantuan hands lost their bloody grip on the splintered remains of the bulwark. Just one blink later, and all that was left of the enormous man were a few bubbles. Olaff was all alone.

Olaff took a shield from one of his dead shipmates and looked around the boat once more. A vein rose to the surface of his neck and then sank. He was just now seeing that these things had killed his shipmates, all of his shipmates. He was angry, so very angry. He was not angry that he was not mighty enough to break their bodies. He was not angry that he was not swift enough to evade their attacks. He was not even angry about what they had done to his companions.

It came from nowhere and consumed him. Hatred and fury ripped at his mind. He could feel the blood rushing hot through every part of his body. His blood felt like a boiling stream he had plunged his fist into. He could hear every beat of his heart thump against his ribs and found it frustrating how long he had to wait for the next one. He looked down at the shield he had meant to protect himself from the world with. He realized the world would need to protect itself from his shield. He looked to his sword wracked by the tremors of a white knuckled grip and saw only his

7

arm. He looked down at the blood washed deck of the Jarl's ship and saw only his own ship painted with honour. He looked at the merfolk, and the various aquatic mer-beasts among them, and saw only sheep.

The fight, if it could be called that, was easy. At first it felt strange he should be able to cut through them so easily. After a few minutes it felt natural, as though that was how it was always meant to be. It confused him that they would choose to move so slowly, but he didn't bother to contemplate it. His brain didn't want to think very much about anything. His arms and feet knew what to do without it.

His eyes were so used to tracking merfolk trying to slither away they almost didn't see the only warrior who stood their ground. The only other soul left on the ship. There was fear in her eyes, but she was no coward. She would not run. Olaff knew she would go to Valhalla when he killed her.

I've never heard of Odin taking mermaids, but he's smarter than me since he's the god of wisdom. He must already know how strong she is.

She stood in a ring of olive green mer blood, where the juice of her honorless allies had been spilled as they attempted to flee. She held her strange weapon in question, the three-pronged tip pointing at the seafarer. Olaff answered her challenge with his own weapon mirroring hers.

He looked at his outstretched arm and saw it was Vjolf's scimitar in his hand. He could hardly recognize it with all the green fluid dripping over its notched back edge. The shield he held was equally alien but he knew from the size it must be Bjorvak's even without the spear tips that had once coated it.

Olaff noticed that the mermaid held two of these odd tridents only after she threw one of them. He was already moving forward when it reached him. He knew there was no reason to avoid it. He had taken more than a couple stabs and slashes so far. None of them seemed to hinder him very much. In truth the only thing that *really* hurt was his splitting headache.

Instead of taking yet another trident to the chest, he slid on his knees under it. The deck was slick enough to travel some distance on the blood of his enemies. With reflexes faster than he had ever possessed, he snatched it from the air with his teeth.

His opponent circled him as he stood, spear still in his mouth. Olaff watched right back with empty eyes as he bit down with all the might of his jaws on the spear. This spear did not give, however. It was not wood or even bone; it was metal. He did not flinch as his teeth cracked and fell with the spear onto the deck, but she did.

He lunged and she stabbed to repel him. He was faster, faster than a viking and far faster than her. Olaff managed to hack thrice before she could withdraw. She tried to force him back again but this time he was ready. He swung the flat of his blade backhanded at her weapon's tip, as if it were a club, and bashed it downwards. Not allowing the opening to pass he jumped, turning sideways and slamming his shield into the spear haft. The weight of his body and the force of the blow snapped her weapon between the shield and the deck. Before he hit the ground he spun blindly, striking at her face with the back of his sword hand. He didn't need to hear the crack over the pounding of blood in his ears to know he broke another tiny bone somewhere in his hand.

They both hit the ground. His head cracked into hers and

9

her head bounced off the deck. Even before they landed, Olaff was already flipping the sword around. He wanted the serrated edge to be facing out. Serrated edges couldn't be used for hacking or slashing, but they were perfect for sawing ropes or throats. One drag across her neck and that would be it. He didn't use the wicked edge, however. Olaff had the sword on the left of her neck. All he would have had to do was rake it across but he stopped.

*Why did I stop? Will the blade not work? No, of course it would. I've seen Vjolf cut plenty of throats with this, it should be **especially** suited for women... Then what's wrong?*

He spent a few moments panting akin to a wolf after a chase. His mind cleared enough for him to realize that her eyes were closed. She was unconscious.

She must have hit the deck too hard...

If a warrior dies without facing his death, with weapon in hand, that warrior goes to Niflheim the afterlife of cowards. Not Valhalla. Niflheim has no water, only ice. She could not swim there. It is a lonely place. Cowards are all that live there and cowards have no friends. Cowards abandon their friends.

She can't go to Niflheim. She wouldn't like it there, she would be lonely. If she dies sleeping she won't see the blade. She won't see her death. I'll wait for her to wake up so I can send her to Valhalla instead.

Olaff got off of her and found a bench. He did not sit down however, he was too anxious. There would be a long wait for his heartbeats to revert back to a steady rhythm. At the moment they were nothing more than an indecipherable stream.

10

To occupy himself he observed the only other living person on the boat. Her hair was red, or maybe just bloody, he couldn't tell. It would have taken blood from many warriors, he knew, to soak such a wild mane. She bore no armor, nor aura of superiority, unlike those she had arrived with. She was not particularly beautiful for a mermaid. He had seen and slain many more gifting to the eye. She was not like all the others he had killed. Looking at her made him happy. It calmed him down.

He started to wonder why Bjorvak hadn't hit him in the nose for not killing her. It would not bother him so much when he did. He knew it was the right choice. He knew Vjolf would be getting the best loot if he didn't start grabbing things now, but he didn't care. All he was concerned about was her anyway. The Jarl would try and claim her as his slave but Olaff would not let him. She was no thrall.

The throbbing in his head subsided and he was able to think more than just basic thoughts. He began to understand a few things. They came to him slowly and eventually. But in the end, he realized that Vjolf, Bjorvak and the Jarl would not do any of those things ever again.

The second thing that he came to comprehend was what he had just done. He was a berserker. He was someone capable of letting the *vauldyr* overtake them and go into a battle rage. Olaff did not know what the "vauldyr" really was but he knew what the effects were. Battle fury, made you feel no pain from weighty flail or jagged knife. It made you stronger than the darkest storm waves and faster than the winds that blew them. Most importantly, as he'd just discovered, it made you struggle to think about anything more than killing.

At first Olaff had thought he was probably just average at

11

going berserk just as he was mediocre at everything else. Then he remembered that only the best berserkers didn't need to drink a potion called the wolf's brew to use the vauldyr. For once, in his entire life, Olaff had something about him that was above average. Even an average berserker is better than an exceptional viking and he was an exceptional berserker. For the first time, however, he didn't really care.

No one would ever know he was anything but normal. Olaff felt wet, and he looked down to see not all of the blood was green, not even half. It hadn't hurt when he was committing heroic acts, but damn, it sure hurt now. His father had told him tales of the things he'd never be, so he knew berserkers healed from most things. His mother had told him tales of the same kinds of things, so he knew that even berserkers died.

He wondered if he would go to Valhalla when he died. The boat would likely sink to the bottom of the sea where the hall of Aegir and Ran was. The warrior thought it possible that *that* was where he was headed. It was where those who died at sea went. Olaff knew he was going to die out here in the middle of a great blue ocean. The hall under the sea was not as good as Valhalla, but it was not bad. He knew he would not die in battle; the mermaid would not wake up soon. He knew this because now that his mind was working properly, Olaff knew clear as northern air that she was not sleeping. She was dead. His previous observation was child like, he realized, as though she were a dog who had 'run away.'

"Dogs don't run away in the north. Not even dogs like the cold enough to starve there." He wheezed, remembering his father's words. He was attempting to gauge how much blood had gone into his lungs. A few red misted coughs later, he wished he didn't know.

*She hit the deck **hard,*** he thought, a stone forming in his throat. ***Really**, really hard.*

Olaff looked at the mermaid and thought his words rather than spoke them. He didn't want to force the words from his perforated lung. past the lump in his throat. Over his tongue lacerated by tooth shards. Out his mashed lips.

You were not the fairest, or the strongest, but you were the only one without armor. You were not afraid enough to run, or brave enough to charge. You stood your ground, gloriously average. You were not afraid of what you were, or what I was: your death... I don't know where I'll go now, but you...you'll

Olaff sat. Thinking was hard again. He punched the thick pine bench hard and broke his hand shut over the grip of his blade. This way he would die with a weapon in his hand. He would not let go. Olaff looked up at the sky, far from bland, and sat up straight.

3 A.M.

3 is the loneliest number. At 12, the people with work the next day are done hanging and head home. At 1 the reckless are partying strong. At 2, you can still find someone to talk to. Friends exist at 2. If you aren't still hanging out at 3, no one wants to start. It's too close to 4. People need to sleep. But I guess I'm not exactly "people."

If there is no rest for the wicked, I guess you can call me Doctor Doom. I'm being facetious, of course. I have no castle in Latveria. No robot army at my command. No, I'm quite alone most of the time. Then again, you don't really understand what "most of the time" means for me. Not yet. Perhaps I should explain.

I don't sleep. Call it my superpower if you like.

I know what you're thinking, and I mean you *are* right. A lot of benefits *do* come along with never sleeping. For one, I'm ripped as fuck. You would be too if you were never tired, and had twice as much time as you do now. Although I suggest budgeting time, because I've never met anyone else like me, and I don't think it's contagious.

That leaves me and crack-heads. Crack-heads are about as

unreliable as well... yeah, crack-heads, so that leaves me alone most of the time. And there's the down side.

Leave a man, who's sad without a reason, alone long enough and he'll damn sure find a reason. If he's clever, he'll find a few. Like any skill, you get better at it with practice. That's when you know you're really in hell. You become your own 3 A.M. warden of a lonely hell all your own.

But I'm not lonely now. I have somewhere to go. Someone will be awake there, breaking the 3 A.M. rule. When people are awake at 3 A.M. and are not getting ready to go to bed, they are in the same boat as me. It's a very lonely boat. Sometimes those sailors want to talk, and sometimes that means I don't have to be lonely anymore, either.

Now, my friend has a name, of course, but you don't need to know it. She is a sweet girl though. So sweet I would have rather been alone than answer the phone to hear her crying. Instead, I was marching in defiance of a dozen orange crosswalk hands toward her building.

For a building with so many people the security is pretty lax. The door PIN is the same as it was back when me and her were a thing. "7-6-6, one away from being the number of the beast" rattled around in my head, knocked loose from a place long abandoned.

As I took the long elevator ride to her floor I thought about our history. Relationships don't come as easily to me as the skills you can learn from how-to YouTube videos. No one can teach me to fall asleep with a girl in my arms. There's no tutorial to show me how to slow my heartbeat to a calm lullaby. In the same respect, no matter how much time someone devotes to me, it'll never really be enough. Even if a girl dedicated half of her waking hours to me, it would only ever be a quarter of mine.

I knocked on her door and reminded myself this was not about my problems. When she answered, I needed no reminder.

I wish I could be a super hero. I wish I could put my hundreds of meticulous hours of knife throwing to the test. I wish I could patrol the streets and beat up "bad guys" who snatch purses and rob liquor stores. But no matter how long one man wanders a city, he just doesn't see any evil to smite.

This was the most good I could do. Listen. And so I did, knowing how long I would hear the story play in my head without pause for sleep.

When it was over, I told her what I thought would help. The truth. "You could not have stopped it from happening."

Unfazed, she kept staring at a full mug of tea gone cold. "Of course I could have. A gun has a shit ton of stopping power. I could have blown the fucker away with the first weapon since the whip to go supersonic. I could have broken the sound barrier using a hollow-point round with a cruciform tip. Do you know what that would do? The round would mushroom and tumble through his innards, tearing them apart. The exit wound would be so big that everyone who saw that unwashed stain on a brick wall in an alley... They would all be thinking the same thing. 'Some shit-head died here.'"

I placed a hand on her arm and lowered the mug to the table. "**You** could not have stopped it. Dirty Harry could have stopped it. Robo-Cop, the Terminator, the Punisher, sure. But you? *You* were not the person to carry around a pistol, with

17

enough kick to bruise a palm, loaded with bullets against the Geneva Convention, and you won't be."

Once upon a time I had spent a lot of time staring at her closed eyes wondering what went on in those blue pools. I didn't need to know her as well as I did to know she was no Judge Dredd. A nose ring and an Iron Maiden tat hardly made anyone a killer anyway.

"You are not about to don a trench coat and start pumping war crimes into swastika laden foreheads. You just won't. It's stupid to change the direction of your life because of this. Think of it like this: The human brain is too complex for us to comprehend it. If it were more simple we too would be simple and thus could not comprehend it. No matter how complex the defense, it is invariably devised by a human, and so all assaults will be brought with equal complexity. The idea of invulnerability is a fallacy. Macs do get viruses. There are no Mario stars to grab in real life," I told her.

She stared absently at the ground as she zipped up a sweatshirt I just began to recognize. "What if I just crawled inside a diamond box?"

"You'd suffocate."

She shrugged again setting her black hoodie loose on her shoulders. "Maybe."

I wondered if she remembered whose sweatshirt it was.

"This did not happen to me because it simply does not happen to everyone. There are not enough bad people in the world for that. Don't envy me though. You know something that many do not. You know you are stronger than most. You are stronger than me. If this had been me, who is to say that I would not have fucking killed myself or something? Who am I to know that? You know something most don't. You know *exactly* how tough you are."

She tugged at her sleeves so that only the tips of her fingers were exposed to the chill of the room.

"I'm sorry I can't be of more help to you. All people can do really is listen and talk about stupid shit and it never helps. People heal their own wounds. No matter how hard I try, I cannot reach into your soul and tear away the sadness."

My palms rubbed hard against my knees as I waited for the wealth of my words to sink in. I watched her zoned-out eyes contemplating and wished I had more to add. You never really *can* say enough, can you?

"So shit happens?"

"...Basically."

"That helps." She stood up. "It actually does."

When I finally left I hoped it had. After I pushed the down button at the elevator bank, I opened my Facebook app to message a friend who is always on for eleven to twelve minutes while he waits for the 5:16 train. I watched that loading screen and envied my ex. She had a reason for all the emotions she felt. People could take some time to talk to her about her problems because they were tangible. Relatable. She could even sleep it off, while I would play The Floor Is Lava with my own loneliness forever.

But when the elevator dinged and the doors pulled open, I got on and went for the ride.

The Smell Of Pirates

The aromas of rum and sweat wafted about him, with blood and black powder just beneath the surface. That balance was subject to change, of course, depending on the ever-changing winds and where they blew him.

This night, the pirate followed the wind on a wandering walk away from the chaos of the tavern. It whistled past his ear and sent a creaky sign swinging somewhere behind him. The cool breeze carried the far more pleasant smell of the sea and chilled the warm sweat about the man. He did not dislike the sensation. After sweltering in the tavern for a few hours, the sight of a full moon and the feeling of some clean air were refreshing.

On this particular evening, the pirate was sharing a street with another sleepless soul. He spied a pale girl in a black dress a few dozen paces beyond him. Not a nightwalker, the dress was too nice. Not an upscale whore either, they stay in brothels.

Noble-born that one. I'd wager that classy gait of hers was born to an etiquette tutor and a manor. Curious sight it is, to see someone with something to lose, and not the means to defend it, walking round here this late...

He shook the thoughts from his head and turned his eye

inward, to planning and scheming. He had career decisions to make and a direction to take.

The pirate heard a footstep join the rhythm. His heart skipped a beat and in half that time his hand reached his under-over pistol. It was a good instinct but unneeded. There was no danger to be found, not for him anyway. A man came into view with nervous hands. He had sprouted from an alley between the pirate and the girl. His sights were not on the pirate but on a particular girl walking in a place she should not walk at a time she should not brave.

She walked unarmed and alone, far in front of the pirate. He had been aboard a boat long enough to grow thirsty for flesh of the more tender variety. Like a white spider skittering across a black sail, her pale skin sliced through the darkness. The girl's pronounced shoulder blades on her slim frame were like anchors, they dragged his eyes down over her whole form. She was too thin for her dress, so it hung low on her. Her hair was money incarnate. Some magic of breeding and grooming gave her full wavy black hair that spilled over her shoulders messily in such a way that none could mistake it for less than art. Art that a noble might pay a steep dowry for, and a thug might go to great lengths to steal.

While the ruffian following her made no sound, his cohorts who leapt out of the alley to grab her certainly did. The black clad pirate slinked quickly to the shadows on the side of the street. His long coat drifted back against his leg before the rest of the gang showed themselves on the street.

The pirate tucked away in the gloom tugged at his beard as he scanned the attackers for weapons. Just clubs and knives between them. Nothing too dangerous. What snared his attention once again was the girl. She whipped her hair around in the struggle like a wild tavern girl dancing on a table past midnight. Her arms looked thin and delicate gripped as they were by the ruffians. The pirate felt a dull pang of annoyance as the glow of moonlight reflected off her skin was abruptly cut off as she was dragged flailing into the shadows. Her muffled screams were given more volume as he hastened step toward the alley.

There's no point. No one hears you scream here. No one wants to.

He rounded the corner with a wide berth. He didn't want to collide with anyone if someone was rushing to the mouth of the alley as a lookout.

With a clear view of the scene, he took long strides toward the fidgeting huddle of thugs. Crossing his chest the pirate's hand dove beneath his coat to grasp one pistol amongst many concealed there. Brass pommel, silver trigger-guard with a vine embossed along it, 11.7 inch polished steel barrel. Finished ironwood stock.

The pirate turned sideways and extended his arm as his thumb found the hammer, keeping his profile as narrow as possible in case of return fire. He squinted, past the glare of moonlight off his pistol, and took aim at the man wrestling with the girls arms and trying to drag her to the ground.

The oh-so-familiar sound of his pistol cocking put a grin on his face once again, like an old friend buying him a drink.

"Sorry mateys, but I wont be having yer seconds," he said, his finger tightening on the trigger.

The first crack sent a ball straight to the man's sternum with a puff of red mist. He dropped the girl hard onto the ground. His back thumped into the wall followed by his head with a smack. The man left a blotch of head-blood and a smear as he slid sideways to the ground.

With a quick pivot and a fluid motion the pirate dropped the spent pistol into an outside pocket and retrieved a new one with his left. The man holding her ankles turned to see the pirate lining up the new pistol with his shoulder. He barely had time to open his mouth before another loud crack split the air and another cloud of unspent powder puffed into the alley.

The thug dropped the ankles, causing the girl to wince once more, and his hands found his neck. Blood spurted from between them. The man blinked away the spots from the bright flash of the pistol before tipping backward and crumpling.

This midnight excursion is turning out to be no fun at all. Lookin' the other way and lit up with moonlight? A bit too easy, this game.

The pirate twirled the pistol around his left index finger and dropped it into a pocket as his right hand went to his belt. The third and final thug turned just in time to see the pirate draw his sword.

Fortunately, I make my own fun.

"En garde, ye scurvy dog," rumbled the gravel of his chest as he drew the blade with a flourish.

You can spend a great deal of time introducing yourself, teaching the fear that should be associated with you, or you can

25

act a familiar role and inherit the fear it bears. And, to the pirate, the latter was far more fun.

The thug had been in the process of drawing a different sort of sword that he was then stuffing back into his pants in favor of one of steel. It was a scratched, dinged thing he drew.

It was a sharp contrast to the pirate cutlass leveled before the man's face. Single-edged, tempered steel curved ever so slightly to a dull brass basket guard over an angled grip fitted with a black leather wrap interlaced with gold wire. The basket was dinged and scratched from noses and teeth, but the blade was clean of significant damage. A fair number of souls had been sent to the bottom of the blue by this blade by the very pirate who wielded it then. He liked his weapon because, like everything good, it cost a lot of money... for whoever actually paid for it.

When the thug yanked his weapon free of its scabbard, it became very obvious his sword skills were more catered to muggings and threatening women than dueling a pirate.

The thug gestured to the girl and opened his mouth, but the pirate cut across his words before more than breath could leave his throat.

"You can give me naught that I can't take," the pirate said sharply as he bent an arm around behind his back like a proper fencer. "And I'll be taking everything mate."

The wit blew right past the alley-man. With his heart beating his arms to a tremble the only thing he could grip was his weapon.

Desperation spurred the thug to lash out. With the pirate's

arm overextended it looked as though disarming him would be easy. This was, of course, a trap. The pirate held his sword with a loose grip which, unlike the panicked death grip of his opponent, would not leave him weaponless come a heavy strike. Instead, the thug's sword skated right off the pirate blade and into the mortar between two bricks on the wall.

The man's eyelids fluttered at the mason dust blasted back at him. The pirate was of the opinion that opportunity is as fickle as the tide, and seeing the opening, he took advantage. With a heavy chop he sent blood and metal to the cobblestones.

Clutching his new found stump, the man hunched over. The pirate didn't watch the sword clatter to the cobblestones, or the man's severed hand spurt blood. Even as the thug whimpered, shrunken and defeated, the pirate wiped his blade clean across the man's back. He had not lived this long in a trade like his without hacking up plenty of people far more deserving of pity than a back-alley rapist.

The bleeding man stiffened and the pirate nearly rolled his eyes. The thug rose, clutching a boot dagger aimed at the pirate's thigh, and the girl squeezed her eyes shut. The sound of a skull being split by an axe was not something she had heard before, and it took her until she opened her eyes to place it.

If a man's got a hand you can't see, best you assume it's clenching a dagger meant for your ribs.

The sound of a sword being driven home to its scabbard drew her eyes away from the face-down corpse with a hand axe in the back of his head. "There are plenty of tricks I've yet to see, but that's not one of 'em."

The pirate had been clutching that axe since he bent his arm behind his back in a mock fencing stance. A simple trick. He had more.

"No need to get up, dearie. You'll do just fine where you are," he told her, his tone suddenly calm and reassuring as he placed a boot on the dead man's back to leverage the retrieval of his axe.

The small, pale girl was anything but reassured. Her hands shook as she adjusted her dress, and her breast quivered with her trembling heart. She was still blinking away the powder's flash. The girl was breathing heavily through her nose in shaky, uneven breaths with no tears to accompany them. She watched him silently with star-bright green eyes.

He took a handkerchief from a pocket on the inside of his coat. He wiped the blood and brain off his axe in no particular rush. She wasn't going anywhere.

Pretty thing she is. Naïve, too, if she didn't expect a scenario of the sort walking around this late in a place like this.

"You had better not be a virgin, lassie. I'll have none of that screaming nonsense," the stranger said in a tone far from humor as his boarding axe was tucked into the back of his belt.

He looked into her eyes hard, but he was the one who looked away first. She was a damsel in distress. A noble's whore or the daughter of one with no marketable skills but earning a dowry, and yet...

A lot of strength in the eyes of a bitch without a gun, or a blade, or blood beneath her fingernails. Why? Who the fuck is she that she can look at me like that? he thought as he squatted down to her level.

He took her by the chin and cheek. He turned her viridian eyes up toward him, and he stared into them.

I want so very much. Money, guns, ships, sex. But looking at those eyes... Now I want something more. But I can't steal this thing I want.

It wasn't merely her eyes, but everything about her. He didn't want to tear her beautiful black dress from her delicate white shoulders. He didn't want to hear her whimper from having her hair clenched in his fist as she was dragged around and bent over. It was something intangible about her that he desired. It confused and scared him so he pushed it from his mind. In its absence, the normal pirate thoughts didn't rush in. He had glimpsed something more, and was too greedy to settle for sex.

She's too damn cute for tears...too bad, too, I bet her ass would feel great against my lap.

A palm, used to taking the kick of pistols, softened for just a moment. He brushed a long lock of curly black hair away from the side of her freckled nose.

"I want you to remember this face."

The pirate's large form blotted out the moon that shone behind him. His shape was outlined in streaking moonbeams that surrounded the girl like timid cage bars. As her eyes grew accustomed to the dark, she began to take in the finer details of his face. A strong jaw beneath a trimmed beard. Greasy black hair that formed tight ringlets tickled at his shoulders.

29

He stood. "Remember it, because if you ever need the help of a pirate," he said, turning back toward the street, "Leon Moriarty will help. And he's the most handsome bastard you've ever seen."

*   *   *   *   *

"Now what was that bilge that came sloshing out of your gullet?"

"None of your business, you sea rat!" spat the man with a broken nose as he leaked some scarlet onto a floor that was in no short company of stains.

"Well, you see," Leon said as he flexed his fingers experimentally. "I happen to be in the business of pretty little alabaster girls. *Especially* when some military big shot has designs on her."

"Pirate!" broke from his lips wetly, as the soldier swung his heavy mallet of a fist.

It was a sure fact that, being accustomed to taverns, Leon was no novice in the art of fist fights. He leaned into the punch directed at his face and headbutted the mans fist. The whole tavern turned to the crack of his knuckles into Leon's forehead just above the pirate's wide, vicious grin.

The soldier staggered back a few steps and cradled his shattered hand. Moriarty laughed, but he didn't follow up on his advantage. He needed information, not bodies.

Another soldier ran at him, fists up. The pirate laughed even harder. A sly boot grabbed a chair from the table behind him and slid it into his legs, knocking him over. Moriarty slapped a hand to the back of his head as he fell and directed his teeth into the edge of a table with a plate-clattering thud.

His mouth closed into a sly smile as he eyed the room, listening to the chairs being pushed out. *Uh-oh...now the tough little tin soldiers are getting serious. Maybe I have to kick the shit out of all of them before they realize I'll fucking kill them all if they don't tell me where the ship is headed.*

The bartender shouted over the clattering of chairs hitting the ground. "Ey you boys! Now you stop this nonsense! I'll have nobody gettin uh killin in 'ere!"

The pirate looked over to see a portly man aiming a blunderbuss uncertainly between everyone involved. An amused eyebrow twitched upward before he could restrain it.

Blast. Should have kept this mess from escalating.

Moriarty put on the worst impersonation of someone who did not murder and steal as a living and addressed the nervous bartender.

"Now, *now*... matey, there's no need to get the scatter shot," he said gently, walking around a table toward the bar.

Those who had previously stood with such fight-ready

31

heads now threw up their hands as they spotted the bold black of the bartender's gun.

"We *gentlemen* are just having some good conversation," he said, walking purposely with a few patrons in between him and the large gun.

The soldiers were still stunned but a few began glancing among themselves.

"Perhaps a bit of good fighting," he suggested, with a mild shrug, sneaking a tankard into his sleeve as he passed a table.

There were some calls for blood and warnings from a few sailors, but they couldn't chip at the mask Moriarty wore.

"Now, *matey*, We didn't mean to cause *concern*," Leon assured, dancing his way dangerously close to the man holding a gun so big it might as well have been a cannon.

Up until the end, Leon's smile persisted, unbroken by the dissonance behind him.

Keeping the bartender's eyes on his face and without drawing attention to the rest of his arm with any excess movement, he flicked the mug at him. Years practicing in sleight of hand flung the tankard harder that most might manage. It flew silently through the stillness of gunpoint and dinged against the barrel of the bartender's blunderbuss. The man jerked his trigger finger, and it blasted a hole in the crowd of patrons beside the pirate.

Without turning to inspect the meaty chunks that had previously been people, Leon closed the distance to the barkeep.

He grabbed the muzzle and jerked it first away and then toward him hard into the man's nose. The pirate slammed it into his face repeatedly until the bartender fell with a mashed nose and less teeth in place than he had woken with.

Moriarty spun on instinct, swinging the heavy metal barrel into the skull of a soldier about to grab him.

Fuck. Now there's what? Three?

Dropping the blunderbuss, his hand dove into his coat and grabbed his favorite pistol. He flicked out the bayonet on the under-over and finished the soldier who'd gone sprawling into the bar stools with a quick jab to the neck.

The pirate whipped around, pulling the hammer back, and saw the last three soldiers running towards the tavern door.

He shouted simply. "It's a double!" then he shot the man in front straight in the head.

The man in the middle saw his head slam into the wall but couldn't stop in time and fell over the corpse. The man in the back stopped in his tracks. Even other patrons stopped fleeing and gave the soldiers a wide berth.

The pirate hopped nimbly onto a table to get a better shot before the last soldier could consider bolting, but the soldier was too scared. He simply turned white and put his hands up in surrender.

"Now then," he said leaping to another table, kicking aside drinks and plates. "what was that captain's name?"

"His name was... Boerand and–"

He tried to pretend he hadn't seen anything but the pirate followed the soldier's gaze to the man who had tripped over his dead companion's body. He was attempting a covert crawl to the door.

When the soldier realized he had been spotted, he scrambled to his feet to cover the last foot to the door. The crack of a new pistol stilled him, however, and the pirate's attention was back on the surrendering soldier. Before he said anything, the silence was broken by the awkward drip of blood falling from his mini bayonet into a mug of beer.

The pirate smiled tightly at his quarry, his pistol still trained on him and a second one smoking in his right hand. "You said Boerand? Where was his boat headed?"

"Look mate, I didn't mean to cause all this trouble. It was just some loose lips I heard about the captain getting his muzzle loaded for some wench with skin as white as a ghost," the soldier whimpered.

"Yes I heard that part when I was eavesdropping," he said hopping once more to a table even closer, spilling drinks and bending cutlery.

"You changed the subject before telling me where the horny fuck's boat was headed. Well I suppose technically you were telling your friends but that's just semantics really," he said with a shrug as he twirled the unloaded pistol and dropped it into an outside pocket of his coat.

He dropped down from the table with a heavy-booted thud and began to saunter over to the soldier. Without even turning his head, he thrust his pistol's bayonet into a man's eye as he passed him. The man's hand dropped from whatever weapon he was trying to pull from behind his back, and he hit the floor with a shocked, strangled scream through clenched teeth.

The soldier squeezed his eyes shut and recoiled turning his face away. "Okay, okay! He said they were to sail for Ceasura through the Pitalis Current!"

The pirate threw on a grin and began walking, past the soldier on the sailor's right, towards the door. "Well, then, I say good day to you mate. I quite enjoyed our little conversation. Just remember if Leon Moriarty ever asks you to 'please repeat what you said,' you fucking do it so he doesn't have to–"

His sentence died in his throat, and he leveled his pistol at the door. The soldier to Moriarty's right slowly opened his eyes to see his superior officer holding a bouncy gun.

The pirate was familiar with this type of weapon. It had a soft shell that only exploded after bouncing around the deck two or three times, or at least that was the idea. The round that was designed to blast a hole in the deck also tended to explode on impact with someone's chest to create much more than a hole in their body. It was a dangerous, unpredictable weapon and was rarely used.

The grunt saw the firing mechanism was pulled directly back to spear through the center of the flint ring as soon as he let the trigger swing forward. The soldier began backing away from the man about to be turned into meaty chunks.

The corner of Leon's mouth twitched in a smile. "You know, pointing a gun at a pirate is a dangerous career move for a soldier, even if it is a dead man's swing."

"Pointing a pistol at a soldier is a bad life decision for a pirate."

The soldier to Moriarty's right reached for his pistol far too slowly. The pirate whipped out another flintlock with his right hand and shot him in the chest without turning his head.

Despite the loud clattering of the corpse getting blasted into the table and then knocking over several chairs on its way down to the floor, the artillery-wielding lieutenant's finger did not loosen on his trigger. He just kept on staring down the barrel at the pirate in front of him.

Cool head for a military man. He won't waste his shot. My options are surrender, or...

"You know," Leon began, replacing the smoking pistol with a fresh one from inside his coat.

"I heard from a fellow, a particularly *loud* fellow," he continued, flipping the bayonet back under the barrels of his favorite pistol.

"This fellow, you see, said he bounced a bouncy charge off his cock, right back onto an enemy boat's deck," Moriarty said, tossing the double-barrel pistol up in the air while keeping the spare centered on the officer's chest.

"I said he was a liar," Leon said, catching the pistol by the barrel as though readying to pistol whip.

"But now that you've got it all ready and loaded... I figure this," he said gesturing with his head towards his pistol, "has got to be at least as hard as his dick was that day." he said gently un-cocking the spare pistol and stuffing it into his coat.

*   *   *   *   *

The captain shook the thick, soggy paper until it ripped. The warrant was useless anyway. The picture was a runny mess.

"I know one of you is the girl I'm looking for. The sooner I find out which one that is, the sooner we can all get on with our lives," the captain said, genuinely trying to restrain his underlying anger at the situation.

Unaware of how close the lava was to the surface, one noble's daughter flicked a long blonde curl so it rested between her breasts. The key to most of her problems could be solved by reminding people of the grandeur of her bust. She interlaced her fingers in her lap, and straightened her elbows to push her diplomats up.

The silence was only broken by the creaking of the ship, as it swayed dangerously up and down in the rough current. An antique chandelier clinked its glass hangings together, and they all heard something roll and then fall with a solid thud.

The blonde one glanced at the other girl to see if she was going to speak. She wasn't. "I can assure you commandant, my father is a very wealthy merchant and loyal to the emperor. In fact he is a personal friend of admiral–"

"Shut the fuck up!" snapped the captain. "I don't *care* who your father is!" Each word came out trembling with emotion in a tone barely creeping above a whisper.

The commandant took a breath and then let it out. With a gentle, trembling hand he slowly slicked over his already smoothed-over hair.

He addressed them with averted eyes and shallow breath. "Alright, I'm going to leave you two young ladies in the comfort of my quarters," he said swallowing, causing his prominent Adam's apple to bob. "And hopefully, you can think long and hard about what you'll tell me tomorrow," the captain said calmer than before, complete with a very forced smile.

He made his way to the door and half turned. "I also hope you don't decide to waste even more of my valuable time."

Waste his time? the raven haired girl wondered as the door closed. *Once we reach port he'll be able to establish our identities, and more importantly his quarry. He doesn't need information from us. He needs to know what that paper said. The bastard doesn't even know who he's looking for, and that's his fault. He should have at least glanced at the thing before leaving suspects alone with his only copy.*

The pale girl turned toward her fuming companion, and the sudden source of aghast vitriol spewing from her perfect lips. *Look at her, so upset about this mix-up that's cost her the last few days of her vacation. She's no right to moan to me of her troubles, of the agony she feels having to return home so soon... If only she knew what perspective meant.*

*　　*　　*　　*　　*

Moriarty was laughing so hard he was near stumbling. Over his laughter he could scarcely hear the screaming chaos behind him. The tavern was in flames. Gunpowder and liquor burn hot. Some ran bloody, with singed clothes and smoky lungs from the place. Others ran towards it with futile buckets.

With no particular haste, he walked right from the waterfront tavern to a merchant standing in front of his boat with brilliant fire mirrored in his spectacles. His mouth open in a frozen gasp of horror.

A flaming timber hit the ground with a loud smash sending smoking splinters across the cobblestones. "WOOOH! That is how you make yourself some **fun**, my good man!" the pirate said, blowing an ember from his jacket with a loud whistle.

The businessman looked nervously from pirate to burning inn and back to pirate, now much closer. He blinked up at the tall man, eyes large through the magnification of his glasses.

"What be you transporting there?" the pirate asked, putting his arm around the pasty man and ushering him along for a walk down the dock.

The merchant hesitated, eying the pistols visible inside the pirate's coat. "I-I sell oil for lamps up and down the–"

His words were cut off by being swung off the dock and into the water with a mewling splash.

39

Moriarty grinned at his good fortune as he clapped his hands clean of soot. "Not on my new boat, you don't."

His left hand tossed his coat back from the hilt of his sword as the sea wind took it with his hair and blasted them both behind him. *Now to inform the crew...*

*   *   *   *   *

The dark-haired girl had spent hours with her face in her hands, trying to find a way out of her predicament. These hours had long past, however. Now she lay on the guest bed in captain Boerand's quarters with her hands interlaced behind her head.

"I'm rightly fucked," she sighed.

A sharp gasp caused her to jolt with fright. In truth she had forgotten the blonde girl was even in the room, or else her heart would not be pounding quite so hard.

"You call yourself a lady!? And you speak such vile terms in open air? Why, you sound like a-an awful pirate with a mouth so vile."

The raven haired girl sat up quickly with a flutter of her eyelids, lips pursed and her head cocked to the side. "Firstly, I never called myself any type of lady. In fact I would call myself *and* you a **girl**, seeing as you look about my age. Secondly, I don't see anything so terrible about a pirate."

The blonde girl gasped again. The pale girl's eyelids fluttered and then shut as she pursed her lips. She breathed in a breath meant to inspire patience and tried to drown out the other girl so she wouldn't be tempted to literally drown her.

"How can you not see anything wrong with piracy!? It is a vile and horrible practice of taking that which is not yours and telling all else that it belongs to you when it most certainly does not."

"Shhhhh!" cut the black-haired lass through the other girl's droning lecture.

Before the aghast noble's daughter could voice her outrage at having been shushed the pale girl waved her to silence with a frantic gesture. "You hear that?" she hissed.

Muffled shouting invaded the moment's hush. Before the blonde girl could protest, the raven-haired prisoner made her way to the door. She opened the door a crack to check for guards, but there were none. Everyone was watching something off to the right of the door. She slipped out to see what the door had been hiding.

When she stepped out, she saw a terrifying and amazing sight. Sailing towards the ship, on black waters, was a vessel awash in blood and fire. Impaled on the bow was a headless, flaming corpse and hanging from the crow's-nest were at least three crew members with their legs missing, open arteries painting the mast. What illuminated the whole gory scene, however, was what really caught the girl's eye. It was a Jolly Roger artfully drawn in fire across the sail.

Looks like a bunch of blokes that grew from dull kids. The opposite of what anyone tells you to do is always the best thing to do. None of these sailors were rebellious enough as kids, or they'd know that. If they had been, they wouldn't be looking starboard right now. I've never seen such a bold demand to "look over there." Of course given my current situation, I can't think of a reason not to bump the table. Hell considering the dice, I might as well flip the table. Nothing in it for me to point out–

Her thoughts were roughly interrupted by the firing of the starboard cannons. The sudden shift threw the sea-legless girl from her feet. When she had blinked the dots from her eyes, she sat up and saw a giant piece of timber impaled into the blurry glass window of the door she had just gone through.

"*...Shit...*"

"That is no language for a young lady to be using," came a voice from behind her.
She looked around to see the military captain's sour face illuminated by the burning ship. "You, little miss," he said re-slicking his hair to one side, "are supposed to be in my very generous accommodations."

Boerand completely forgot about being furious with the girl as soon as he saw his very expensive window shattered by debris from the ship he had just ordered his men to fire on.

The man went over to inspect the damage just as the ship rocked from a second round of shots. He stumbled and nearly impaled himself on the wooden spike.

"Almost..." the girl mumbled a bit too loud, and two bits too wistfully.

The commandant whipped around so fast his hair flopped out of place, yet again.   She noticed, to her dismay, for the first time in the new fiery light that he was holding his saber in a white-knuckled grip that caused the whole sword to tremble.

Shit. He heard me.

"I just, um, meant, uh... that it is too bad that the splinter did not hit the person who fired the shot that broke your window," she said, trying desperately to keep her voice from shaking.

He barely heard her fearful response. Instead, he tore the door to his cabin open, dislodging the piece of smoking tinder and some remaining bits of glass to the deck. "Get the fuck inside," he said in a dangerously low tone, smoothing his hair over with a shaky hand. "And stay there."

She hurried inside without protest. The door slammed shut, grazing the tail of her dress and showering glass about her. She calmly walked to the bed, remembering the same previously near useless etiquette lessons that had let her calm her voice moments before.

"I told you not to go out there," said the blonde girl in a matter-of-fact tone of voice.

Never had such a short sentence made the girl so endlessly angry. "You didn't say *shit,* so shut the **fuck *up*!**"

Her breath came back to her ragged after that outburst. Steady breathing did not return to her with ease either. Perhaps it was the obvious rage that did it. Maybe the fear beneath the surface from her encounter with the commandant. Or maybe it was the frustration that persisted beneath it all. The frustration at being dragged back to a life she went to such lengths to leave. But then she knew that she shouldn't be surprised. A life in a mansion gives you the imagination and knowledge to escape it, but apparently, not the experience to get very far.

Finally, she's quiet. She lay back on the bed once more. *I just hope she stays that way. For her own good.*

*   *   *   *   *

*Why don't **I** have one of these **this** nice?* Moriarty asked himself as he looked at the bloody boarding axe in his hand.

He snatched up a head rag from one of the fallen cannoneers and leaned his sword against the wooden partitioning wall between two cannons.

*It **is** a nice chopper, so I might as well clean it off if I'm going to keep it.*

Once the axe was free of brains and blood, he belted it. Leon snatched his sword up before the rocking of the ship succeeded in sending it clattering to the floor. The pirate made his way to the first stall and kicked over the powder barrel.

Now how did that song go again?

"One, and, two, and, three, and, four, and–" With a strong kick he rolled a barrel to one side of the deck.

He continued down the line humming his favorite tune as he directed all the powder barrels to the port side of the ship. He didn't lose the beat as he sheathed his sword and took out the oil-soaked rope from a leather sack in his coat. He arranged the enormous coil in complicated knots to each barrel so they would all ignite at the same time. When he was done, he wiped his hands on a rag and admired his handiwork.

Now for the second verse. The creaking wood and the low muffled whistle of ocean wind was interrupted by a quick scrape. Where none dared bring a lantern he held a match

Shadows trembled for a moment before the match fell, and then fled. "A one, and a two, and a three, and a four, and a one two three four," the pirate counted off as he walked to the door with a spring in his step.

I'm gonna have a good bit of fun here.

A short while later the pirate swung the door to the deck open and the chef's head rolled out a crimson carpet for the singing pirate. As he stepped through the portal onto the deck, he tapped his blade against a lamp like a bell, as though entering a shop. Instantly, they were all hypnotized. All eyes were upon him, but no one moved. In a trance of indecision, they watched the tip of his sword as he moved it about like a conductor's stick.

They all boast about in the tavern. About how much fun they would have if a pirate ship were to try something against their fleet. But they don't know what to do when one walks onto their deck singing? Sorry sods, this lot.

Moments later the spell was broken by frantic shouts of action from behind him at the bow. He twirled around, acting like a drunkard, and spotted the captain. Moriarty just kept on singing as he observed a very upset captain throwing his maps and charts at his closest underling in frustration.

*Uh oh Mister Important looks **rather** upset.*

The pirate made his way toward the middle of the ship, nearing the end of his song.

The crew members were slow to react, but captain Boerand was not.

"Never mind, you *fools*! I'll kill him myself." shouted the captain, thundering down the wooden steps to the deck.

The soldiers loosely surrounded the pirate, unsure of how to act until the captain yelled for one of them to fetch his rifle.

"Well, well, if it isn't a mad pirate," Boerand said, slicking his hair over again. "You have your sword drawn, little singing monkey. Does this mean you wish to duel with I? I am a master fencer as well as–"

In an exaggerated, dancing pirouette, Moriarty whirled around and threw his sword at the mast directly behind him. It stuck there, quivering, a quarter of the way up the wooden pillar.

He turned around with a broad smile, singing his song in a low tone, "*because I am a pirate and–*"

"Your rifle, Sir?" offered an uneasy underling.

"If you refuse to act like a man, I'll shoot you like a dog," Boerand said, sheathing his sabre.

"*I know about the cannons,*" he sang on, unfazed, with a glint in his eyes that made the captain itch to put a ball between them. The captain snatched the rifle with his jaw clenching and unclenching.

"If there's anyone to ask, who'll tell ya bout the gold," he sang on defiantly, even as a vein bulged above the sights of the officer's rifle.

Before the captain could bring his finger inside the trigger guard, the swashbuckler's voice rang out in one more lyric. *"**But only the dead can tell you bout the–**"*

An explosion rocked the ship. Moriarty took a few steps backward as though allowing a dance partner to take the floor. The wooden world they inhabited warped. Wood and water exploded to the sky, and the ship lurched sideways. The floor rejected the crew, and they were embraced instead by the waves. Amongst the panicked screams and splashes, a soft tune could be heard whistled within the chaos. Moriarty, having timed the explosion perfectly, was ready, and his steps backward had transferred him from the deck to the – now sideways – mast, with hardly a stagger to his step.

Boerand was lying belly down across the mast now, with the whole of his front side stinging. With his rifle surrendered to the depths he pushed himself up to his hands and knees. With blackness encroaching on the walls of his sight, he looked up and saw the word "boom" mouthed silently, finishing the song. All the sounds of chaos can seem so far away in the ring after an explosion. The sound of two pistols being drawn could have been a step away in a quiet room. The familiar click of them being cocked back could have come from a breath past his ears.

Boerand scrambled in vain to stand, but before he made it past his knees, he heard two cracks and froze. He looked at his white tunic, blinking away the spots, and saw no red. A moment later he heard two splashes.

The pirate had shot two of his men clinging to the rigging and dropped them into the sea below. The flintlocks spun round his fingers and were shoved deep into his coat into some hidden pair of pockets. Graceful as a swan, the pirate plucked his cutlass from the mast and tossed it to his left hand.

Few people ever fight a left-handed swordsman, and I bet he hasn't either, Moriarty thought, eyeing the blade on the soldier's right hip. *Nothing fucks up a lefty like fighting another lefty.*

Moriarty moved the tip of his sword in a half-circle and cut the air downward with a satisfying, high-pitched whoosh that only the sharpest of blades can make.

With no mirth or merriment of song, the pirate scraped a gravelly: "En garde" from his throat.

Boerand finished scrambling to his feet and ripped his sword-belt off of his waist. The hard scabbard was yanked off his cutlass and then discarded to the waking water below.

The commandant hefted a sabre in the moonlight. It was more curved than Moriarty's cutlass and so allowed for better slashing and maneuverability amongst the rigging of a ship. In exchange, he sacrificed the range Leon would have along with a greater ability to thrust.

Boerand was uneasy about entering combat on the side of the mast of a sinking ship, but he did not dwell on it. He didn't ponder the duration the boat would stay buoyant or look down at the splashes of his screaming crew being devoured by the sharks below. He stared straight ahead at his task at hand.

Moriarty's eyes were not spears to penetrate the farthest depths of humanity beyond someone's eyes, but they went deep enough. Leon knew all there was to know about the part of people he needed to be familiar with. He had reloaded enough pistols and cleaned enough swords that his eyes looked where there were answers to be found. The captain's foot placement showed his stance to be one borne of proper training. Boerand's shoulders told of his experience. Most importantly, the captain's eyes told the pirate that Boerand knew where to look, just as he did.

Moriarty was a great liar in all things, just as he was with a blade. He slacked his shoulders and sagged his eyelids. As with laughter, yawns, and fear, so too is laziness contagious. And Boerand was infected. With little awareness, he mirrored the newly adopted hunched back and drooping sword of the pirate. Somewhere in the back of his mind Boerand relaxed, though Moriarty was quick to remind him that his sword had gotten no duller. Moriarty attacked, and he attacked hard. He was brutally quick with his downward stroke and was met with a panicked block. The captain's mind went blank in the grip of adrenaline. The cutlass crashed down again in a shower of sparks, and some primordial part of the captain's mind told him he would be safe if he blocked high again.

Leon feinted high and then made a flash cut with a snap of his wrist at the soldier's cheek. It bit through his cheek and gave him a line across his molars. Muscle memory led Boerand's sword in a parry, but before he could follow through with a disarm, the pirate answered with a straight punch to his nose. Cartilage gave behind calloused knuckles, and his neck snapped back against the weight of his fist. Boerand staggered back to keep from falling. His eyes teared from the blow to his nose, and he waved his saber around with a trembling panic. Moriarty swatted the weapon around like a cat playing with a string and laughed.

The pirate sniffed the salty air and gave up the chase, letting Boerand stumble back into the deck with a thud. Leon Moriarty spread his arms to his sides and inhaled deeply. Amongst the splashes of sharks and the creaking of a slowly sinking ship there could be nothing more tranquil than Leon Moriarty's smile.

"This is what it is. The very center of my existence. The soul of a pirate like me."

Boerand wiped blood and tears from his face and took a breath through a mouth that shook with fear and rage.

"Some say only a spinning compass can find one. They're wrong. Others say you'll feel its chill in the handle of a knife if you stick it in deep enough and twist. Bullshit," he said, leveling his gaze back at the soldier.

Boerand pushed himself off of the wall and shook his head clear.

Leon pointed left and right with his sword, explaining, "West is blood, east is powder." He swept his sword past his boots. "To the south you smell the sea." Moriarty brought his sword up to cross his face vertically. He sniffed. "North lies the stinging smell of steel sparks. The sweet perfume of a sword fight."

Boerand bared his teeth revealing molars running with blood through his slashed-open cheek. Without deigning to respond to the criminal with words, he spoke through steel. The commandant closed the distance quickly, and between them clattered a barrage of cuts and parrys. Moriarty retreated under the flurry, but the smile never left his lips.

"Something funny about your death, **pirate**?" Snapped the commandant with a jerk of his head to readjust his hair.

Was I laughing? It's been too long since I've had a good duel.

"Must've been your big, goofy smile that sparked my humor."

Before the soldier could chase him to the end of the mast, a chill in his chest gave him pause. Although during their last bout he had felt that every next strike might bring him victory Boerand looked down to see his tunic shredded with tiny cuts.

A fortune teller once told Leon that a thousand words can pass in the silence of a stare. After he had retrieved his coin purse from her bloody, writhing form, he'd told her that her 'wise words' were the only thing stupider than trying to pick-pocket him. But as he watched Boerand's grin tear his cheek wound further open, he thought perhaps the lady might have deserved a coin or two.

The difference between dueling for sport and dueling for blood is that the first strike only decides the victor in the former. Boerand saw in the bits of cloth that drifted toward the water that he was not as skilled as his opponent, but that did not mean he couldn't kill him. There was no reason he couldn't give the pirate a few good hacks while he had a sword buried in his own chest. He had enough blood to spare.

When Boerand charged, however, he did not find himself in a bloody draw. Instead, he found his head bouncing off the mast with an axe in his foot. Moriarty had seen enough crazy eyes to know when to trip someone.

The pirate planted a foot on the flat of the commandant's saber and with two hands rammed his blade through his forearm, nailing it to the mast. Just as Boerand looked up at him, the pirate gave him a hard kick to the ribs. It drove his body off the mast and ground a bloody arc into the wood from his face as he rotated around the sword. With the wet pop of his arm, dislocating from the drop off the edge, gritted teeth turned to a strangled scream and kicking legs. He tried to climb back up but to no avail. He found no purchase on the smooth wood of the mast.

The pirate sighed with closed eyes and turned up his chin at the breeze. Apart from smells, Leon had a fondness for sounds. The clicking of a pistol hammer being thumbed back. The smack of a stray cannonball hitting the water. The deep pop of a cork being plucked from a glass growler. The latter was being robbed of him at the moment by the incessant screaming at his feet.

With cold glass pressed to his lips he tilted the back-end up. He relieved the burn with an exhale that was smoky white against the cold night. "Relax, have a drink," he said in a voice drowned by the screams beneath him.

Flipping the bottle upside down, he doused the fiery roar into a silent, seething hatred. He looked up at Moriarty with one eye clenched shut against the burn of the rum that soaked half of him.

Moriarty set a lazy elbow over the pommel of his sword as an armrest, "Did you know in Rimvar they kill pirates and treasonous sailors the same way? They string them up like you do in the empire, but not from their necks – from an arm or leg instead. Then they burn the sods. They call it lynching too, or at least that's what I heard over a drink someplace moldy." The dry rip of a match being lit punctuated his statement.

Moriarty smiled at Boerand with a face illuminated by fire and whispered. "When you get to hell, you let me know if he was right."

The black-haired girl watched her captor burn. And he burned ever so brightly. Like the sun outshining stars, the night darkened around the writhing form of the commandant. It was not a silent affair, but a man on fire does not always have the lungs to carry the depth of his fury to the ears of his tormentor. When his screams fell away and crackling flesh and whirring ocean winds rose up to Moriarty's ears, he cut the burning carcass loose below the wrist. It was a sudden, brutal motion to one knee as he brought the captain's own saber down on him, and the black-haired girl heard the other girl flinch at the sound.

The pale girl could not understand such an alien reaction to the sudden violence of severing the captain's hand. In her mind it was a belated act of mercy. If the pirate had cut him loose a minute prior, it would have been a blessing.

Numbly she watched Moriarty fling the saber at a shivering sailor clinging to the rigging. When the boy hit the water, there was a brief stillness like a held breath before jaws ripped at him and dragged him beneath the surface.

With a head adrift, she watched the pirate wrench his sword free from where it impaled the dead captain's hand. With a tap of his boot, he sent the limb down to the depths after the commandant. As her mind swam with thoughts, one flooded her.

53

It was not quite the fear of a stowaway reaching port wondering if gallows awaited him. No, her body had robbed her of such sense. Still, his black long-coat was far from shining armor, and she was not in a rush to mistake him for a knight.

In truth she did not know the feeling that gripped her. It had either not visited her heart for long enough to become a stranger, or it had never known her to begin with. She would come to know it well, however, as it never left her. Every day she spent with him she felt it. Whether in waves or in ripples.

A feeling she *could* recognize was that of being exposed. She felt it in the breeze that chilled her white leg in the pale moonlight. When the ship had turned on its side, a lantern had smashed in the captain's cabin and with some quick thinking the girl had smothered the oil fire with her dress. As a result, the fire had burned away far more than even the most scandalous fashion statements would allow. Her leg jutted out from the burned dress with only sparse flakes of ash for modesty. It seemed so alien, even to her. Her leg looked like a visitor from a world apart from corsets and dresses.

The last of Boerand's crew disappeared beyond a smoky blood trail woven between sinking splinters in the depths. As they did, the water began to smooth. For how much her leg reflected its light, her limb might have belonged to a daughter of the moon.

Rather than watch the pirate monkeying through the ropes toward her, she watched the chaos of the tide disperse. The closer the water came to a mirror, the more she was fascinated with her exposed left leg. She had never really examined herself naked, nor anyone else for that matter. And without comparison to judge or having compliments from which to affirm it, she knew she had the most beautiful left leg in the world.

Her calf sprouted from a half-boot, that enveloped a foot which could have fit in a glove, and melded into a smooth knee that had never knelt on anything in her life. Her thigh had too sparse of fat to disguise the shape of its muscles and was so thin a man's hand could have wrapped around it. If she turned just a breath to the side, her waving reflection revealed a contour at her thigh's end that merely hinted at proportions past the new singed fray which caused her cheeks to bloom with a hot pinkness. The perfection of her leg was a discovery of vulgarity that shattered her protective blanket of decency and set her heart pounding against the soft lace of her corset. The heat of her body made the ocean breeze sweeping under her skirt and across her exposed shoulders carry a chill she had not felt prior. She could have shuddered, but instead she basked in the goosebumps that rose across her pronounced collarbone and down her jutting shoulder blades.

Though she had scarcely known it to be hers before that night, it was in that cold which penetrated her clothes to their depths that she decided this immaculate leg was hers. It did not belong to her father or the husband he had arranged for her, and it never would. It belonged to her more than anything she had ever owned, and she would not give it away like empty smiles at a party or shallow compliments at a dinner.

She realized this just as the boots of a man that could take anything from her thudded down on the door frame before her. She backed away from the threshold and gave him room to enter. When his boots thudded down into the cabin, the black-haired girl was suddenly reminded that she was standing on the walls. Perhaps the concept of a sideways room was silly in some childish corner of her brain or maybe that bearded smile was a touch contagious. Like a glare off a wave, a laugh, or a smile, or something merry passed through her. For just a blink, the pirate's grin seemed a shade lighter than sadistic.

"Absolutely unacceptable! The level of barbarism! Entering a proper lady's quarters without permission is answerable with a lashing. I should think it unnecessary for someone of such a station to have to remind the likes of you of this."

Is that the sound of madness?

The pale girl did not realize how creaky the walls were to tread on until that moment. His boots were heavy on the old boards. The black-haired girl did not turn as he passed her on the left, but her toes curled when the tail of his coat brushed against her bare leg.

When he was close enough to smell the blonde's perfume without sniffing, he broke his silence. "Pardon?" ground his rough voice into their ears. "You speak of some station, yet I find myself *shamefully* unfamiliar."

She took in a shaky gasp that was meant to be composed. She tried to speak with an air that she could not keep in her lungs. "My father is a powerful man and he–"

His raised eyebrow was enough to cut her off under the weight of the situation. "Power? What power is that?"

She could form no retort. In fact the only sound that came from her was the cascading twangs of her corset laces being severed as he slowly lowered his blade. He stopped halfway down the corset with the tip resting an inch into the flesh below her sternum. She gasped in a breath and didn't use it to make another

56

sound. The girl's contracted chest and half-severed laces worked in concert to drop the garment, allowing two large, heavy breasts to flop free. But his eyes held no fancy for her golden skin stretched over the bottom of her ribs.

The pirate lazily rolled his head around to look at the girl he had come for. "I'm an evil man. There's not enough shades of gray to paint me anything but black. But I like you more than most. That's why you aren't on your knees right now. I'm here to rescue you, in fact, but don't mistake me for a hero. If you come with me, I cannot promise you'll be walking a wise path. I've no inkling how safe you'll be... even from me. I haven't done so much for my own mother that I've got myself doing for you, but that may not last till the wind changes." The words spilled quickly from the lips of a man who did not carry himself like he took a particular haste to his words often.

It might have very well been more truth than the liar had told to even himself, but an honest dog still bites.

Her eyes, bright like an emerald moon, were not an easy place to escape from and she locked him there, unblinking, for the eternity of a breath. "It'll be safer than a sinking ship."

SoulMates

"You were always arrogant. *Cassandra,* mommy's little angel; always seeing reality with a fairy tale filter. I waited for you to grow up. I always hoped when you got to be my age you would see the world for what it was, cold and cruel. Turns out all you needed to see the truth was a little push. Who knew the push had to be your big sister ratting you out to the alderman? *Now* there isn't a sparkle in those big cute brown eyes of yours."

There was a fire behind Cassandra's glare, but she could breathe none of it into speech. Her jaw was nailed to her upper mandible with iron bolts, heavy enough that looking up at her big sister took effort.

"You know they'll throw rotten things at you. That's the punishment for being a **whore,** *Cassandra.* You know they wouldn't have to burn you like a goat fucker if you could have just kept your lips on a nice baker, or farmer but *nooooo.* You had to go off and slobber on a vagrant necromancer. It's *disgusting* really."

Her sister's insults did not sting like they used to. When a hot iron rod is used to restore one's chastity, being called a slut is not so dreadful.

"Where is he now? Hmmm?" her sister inquired, bringing her ear within a tempting distance. "He took your virginity, and what did he leave you with? Not your family. Not your honor.

59

Was it a flower? A poem? It certainly wasn't those." She cackled pointing at the rough blackened circles on Cassandra's chest, where wounds had been cauterized after her breasts were ripped off.

The cruel big sister's eyes were only pushed open by the tears of pure joy she shed from the hilarity of her own joke. They went wide when she felt an icy grip slap across her bony wrist. Cassandra had not eaten anything since her jaw was bolted, but her sister had been feeding the flames of her hatred for the last hour, and that was more than enough to run on. Her big sis nearly lost her footing when she was dragged into the bars. When they heard the crunch of a nose and the crack of a few teeth they saw each other with new eyes. Tattle-tailing had never led to more than a harsh word or a switch across the nose. Their fighting had never caused more than a bruised pride or a pink cheek. Now everything was different. Now Cassandra marveled at how many times she could smash her sister's face into the bars of her cell in such rapid succession.

It was happiness. It was strength. It was more of both than she could remember having no matter how far she looked back. It did not help to squint.

Unfortunately it was also brief. Guards were trying to drag her sister away from the cell. They would succeed. No matter how strong Cassandra felt in that moment, she was not.

Cassandra stumbled slowly backwards into the cell wall, from the force of being torn apart from her. Her sister fell to her hands and knees, and a patter of blood drops hit the dungeon floor. Concerned guards went from scowling at the prisoner to huddling around the injured girl. A hand recoiled from her back as she coughed a blood spray onto the stone. Three teeth fell from her sobbing lips, and Cassandra felt pride. She smiled and leaned heavily on the wall.

Not bad for a country girl, huh?

One of the men must have seen her expression and found it displeasing, for the clank of a gauntlet against rusted bars rang out harshly against the stone walls. Cassandra was beyond flinching. She knew she was in no danger. They would not kill her yet. She was to be burned, and burnings happened at night. Fire was brightest in the dark, and there was nothing but the crackling of flames for her screams to compete against beneath a starry sky.

While her soul was fed on vengeance, legs require food and water. She began to slide down the wall on trembling legs that folded under her.

If I've one regret, it's that I didn't snap her arm over the damned bars, but I'll never regret him. They'll never convince me that love, of ours, wasn't worth anything. Maybe, it's worth more to me than it should be, but it's all I've got, and they won't take it, Cassandra reflected from the piss-stained floor of her cell.

Her body, having long abandoned its duties, beckoned her mind along. Cassandra's eyes were the last to succumb, closing on the dreadful cell and opening instead into dream.

She dreamt of corpse flowers and singing spirits. She dreamt of graveyard picnics. She dreamt of introducing him to her great, great, grandparents. She dreamt of dancing in a ghost ball in a ruined manor.

She dreamt of a boat ride on a moonless night. His skeleton minion rowed them out to the center of a lake, still as glass. Bright spectres flew through the air and water without pause and sung songs in a language long dead. Once far enough out, the minion slipped into the water and walked along the bottom back to shore to give them privacy. The frogs and crickets fled from the ghostly symphony, leaving the lovers in silence. The spirits left at his command, leaving them in darkness. With the boat set to a gentle spin, he bade her look up. The necromancer showed her how bright the stars could be if left alone to shine.

They lay there watching the stars, until the morning mist engulfed them, and will-o-wisps led them back to shore. It was there by that willow tree that they kissed first. He held out a hand at the water's edge to help her off the boat, and she leapt into his arms, afraid he'd never have the courage. He fell backward onto a bed of thick river grass wet with dew, and they laughed. She kissed him beneath those dancing will-o-wisps. She had to be back to her bed by sunrise, but she lingered on his lips a long while...

Cassandra woke drowning. She coughed and gasped as best she could without being able to move her jaw, and eventually she was breathing easily. The liquid was sweet on her tongue. Sugar water. She blinked a man into sight holding a cup. He looked sympathetic, but that hadn't stopped him from peeling back her lips and pouring the drink past her mess of cracked and missing teeth while she slept.

They want me nice and lively for the pyre.

"It's time."

She found the polished boots of the constable and followed the pristine clothes to the face of her fate. He must have forgotten. He did not need to address her. It had been a long time since she was human in the eyes of anyone, including herself.

She was taken outside by stronger men than necessary. She was bound by ropes thicker than necessary. The constable made a stronger case for her death than was necessary. She did not care for her life anymore. They could have it.

"No one is coming to save you, **bitch**." The constable spat as his men doused her in lard.

She had a little corner of her heart that she held the hope for rescue in. She wished for a knight in shining armor. If she closed her eyes, she could see his black cloak billowing from behind his nightmare.

"He's a few days dead now." She shivered from the cold lard. "The sod took a bolt sneaking around town after you were arrested," he said with a soft chuckle. The constable leaned in, bringing the heat of the torch with him. "He right turned to dust at the touch of the swift justice of my guard."

Her face was masked by her matted and knotted hair plastered to her face by the lard dripping down her head. One eye saw out from the mask of hair and stared back at the alderman. Her eyelid fluttered, and he smiled with satisfaction

Glaring would be the tamest word for how she looked at the man. It lasted only a moment before the hot metal of the brazier connected with her cheek, the flesh there hissing and bubbling from the heat. The fat ignited all over her in an instant. She wished she could stare at the constable, simmering with the hatred in her heart for him, but she screamed. If ever the thought that being tortured with hot irons would give her the constitution to resist being burned alive, the notion was quickly vanquished.

Hatred and defiance did not give her the strength to withstand the agony of being immolated. She screamed and flailed, muffled and bound, and if she would have lived any longer, the pain would have reduced her further.

Death was not so scary. Dying was, of course, but death felt like a lover's embrace. It took a kiss on the crown for her to see that it *was*.

"You're safe in my arms now, Cassandra. You need not tremble so." he whispered.

She felt his breath against her hair. It was a light puff, and accompanying it was the softest, warmest voice she had ever heard.

"Is this the next life?" she murmured back into his tunic, with lips that hadn't spoken in far too long.

She could feel cool crypt air. Not the scorching, smoky air of a pyre. This was not the same place she had been a terrible moment before.

"This is my home. You're alive, Cassandra."

She could feel welcome warmth from his hands and a tender binding from his arms. This would have made an afterlife fine beyond any imagining she could have conceived of.

What she thought she had lost forever she clung to then. She found her hands climbing up his back, sliding over soft cloth. Her fingers curled, gripping his shirt, and she nuzzled her face in tighter to his chest. "They said you were killed."

"I'm a lich, Cassandra. I placed my soul in a phylactery in case something were to happen. Destroying my body should have caused me to reform beside my soul jar instantly, but instead I reconstituted into flesh once you, too, had your mortal form obliterated. It doesn't make any..."

He trailed off, and a warm hand left her back. Cassandra dimly heard the soft clink of a necklace chain against stone. "Ah, it *does* make sense. Your soul and mine... they bonded together, within my phylactery. It seems we're soul mates, love." He set the amulet down, and his hand set itself on her back once again.

"I *knew*–" She paused for a shaky breath. "I never doubted there was a good reason you never came," she said, punctuating with a hot sigh into his chest.

"Cassandra, darling... They hurt you, didn't they? The townsfolk, they killed you because of *me*. I'm so sorry. I wish I could–" His words found pause as he swallowed away the lump in his throat.

She could feel his pounding heart and hear the stone in his throat. She held up a soft thumb to his lips to silence his stumbling speech and straightened up to reach his ear. "Kill. Them. *ALL.*"

Amorphous

Chapter 1: Tutti Frutti

I'm always so disheveled in the morning, he thought, adjusting his teeth like beads of an abacus. Each one clicked into place perfectly. Then he took the soap dish and gave a few teeth a good whack.

No one's teeth are perfect.

Today his body was fitted perfectly to his suit. The material felt pleasantly cool against his skin, as he straightened his tie and flattened down creases. His appearance was always key. Nothing could be askew. His head was smooth, devoid of any scalp stubble. Hair was unnecessary, an unneeded complication. A bald head implied age without wrinkles. Wrinkles, too, were a difficulty he would rather forgo.

He cracked his neck left and then right, and exited the hotel room bathroom. All five stars of the Oceanbrook hotel could be found in their king-size beds alone. A king could fit several queens in a bed such as that, without a need for space in the pursuit of princes. Normally his bed is consumed by a writhing mass of flesh, but this morning it lay vacant, still ruffled from the hot skin that it occupied the night before.

67

He made his way to the mini-fridge and took a knee to the carpet before it. Beside the device lay the previous contents of the fridge. Candy bars, alcohol of various types all from the minibar, even the shelves had been pulled from their slots with enough force to break the frost that bound them. None of these things interested him, of course. He opened the fridge to reveal his breakfast: an 84 oz tutti frutti slushie.

He touched his hand to the bottom of the fridge, to cool it, before taking the drink. Melting the slush to syrup before it could be consumed in its proper form, was a terrible shame to behold. He reached for his breakfast and caught a glimpse of his watch, as his sleeve shied from his wrist.

8:17, three minutes until 8:20. It's time to go, if I am to adhere to the schedule. Schedules are important. They keep one's self organized, for this sort of work.

He picked up his breakfast, collected his briefcase, and left the hotel room, slurping all the while.

The patterns on the carpet are so terribly boring, he thought to himself as he made his way to the elevator bank. *I suppose they must be just so. It would be strange to have an exceptionally intricate pattern on the floor. This hotel must abide by the rules and conform.*

He squatted and elbowed the "down" button, to ensure his lips would not have to part from his delicious beverage.

Such a job must be awfully boring. No race but man can create like they do and yet so many find themselves in such pointless existences. Must be terribly unfulfilling to go to art school and aspire to create great works just to have your aspirations stepped upon. Still, I'm sure the artist made a great deal on a hotel chain buying his pattern. Probably has a family to provide for. Christmas gifts to buy, bills to pay. He has people depending on him. He has a purpose to drive him through his work; a far better one than boredom.

At 8:20 the elevator dinged, and his contemplations fled. In front of him stood Giovanni Montecello of the Montecello family and Vinny Petroso, his bodyguard. After a short pause, the bald man entered the elevator, briefcase in hand.

He paused long enough before turning around to cause the bodyguard to uncross his arms. When the bald man placed his briefcase on the floor and pressed the "close door" button he smiled. In doing so, his lips never left the cold, sugary treat in Franko Montecello's hand.

He could hear the stifled laughter of the two mobsters behind him begin, and he felt his right sleeve tighten over his bicep. It was likely very humorous to find a man in a tailored suit drinking a large, pink slushie. He could feel his skin tense as veins surfaced on the underside of his right forearm.

"What flavor you got there, buddy?" asked a smirking Giovanni from behind his muscled wall.

Ah, I see. The liquid is pink, thus I am gay. This is quite humorous.

The only sound that came from the bald man was the hollow slurping noise of a cup, empty save for the last few precious drops. They didn't know this, but that noise was their death knell.

The bald man's smile separated from the corkscrew straw, as the plastic cup fell from his lips, all the way to the floor of the elevator. He cracked his neck to the left – his right deltoid grew in mass just as the triceps and biceps of his right arm had. He cracked his neck to the right – his pectorals joined the rest in making the suit rise on his form.

If the bodyguard had noticed, he certainly had no time to react before the assassin spun, backhanding him. The blow knocked his teeth at the elevator wall, like dice over a craps table. The hit must have felt like a sledgehammer to the face. This was likely because the assailant's hand was now a literal sledgehammer head.

The fore-swing broke the Italian man's skull before embedding the gelled head in the opposite wall. It cracked the mirror wall all the way to the floor. The muscled man remained rooted, until the postmortem spasms from his injured brain shook his broken form to the floor, in a puddle of cranial blood.

Laughter: it makes the heart beat quick. Disrupts breathing. Punctuates sentences. Seals connections between two or more humans within a social interaction. This makes it functionless to me, and yet I find myself partaking now, It thought as It pressed the "emergency stop," bathing them both in red emergency light. It had not turned to look at the panel nor had It taken a step back to reach it. Its eyes were all committed to Giovanni now.

A common misconception is that the "emergency stop" alerts emergency personnel. It does not. There is a second button with a bell icon for that. The "emergency stop" button is, in most cases, characteristically sticky for this reason.

I believe irony is present. as one might say: "You are about to get 'fucked'"

A jab closed the last inch between the mobster and the back wall of the elevator. The cartilage of his nose was smashed completely back into his skull and his mandible was cracked in three places. Blood flooded his sinuses and, as any liquid would, it overflowed anywhere it could find an exit; namely his eyes.

The being before Don Montecello comprehended all of this. The human anatomy was something It had an intimate understanding of.

It opened the briefcase on the floor slowly enough that the mob boss might have asked what lay within if he could have spoken. When the body loses one pathway for breathing, its natural interpretation is the sensation of being strangled; without, of course, the actual loss of air. When he wasn't coughing up excess blood flowing down his throat, Mr. Montecello could breathe. Adequately.

With the hands of Franko Montecello, It pulled a sledgehammer from the black briefcase. Of course the creature was not Franko Montecello. The creature did not have the face of Franko Montecello nor did It have the legs or organs of Franko Montecello. Those belonged to Franko Montecello, who was still very much asleep on Floor 14. He'd had a rendezvous with a beautiful Sicilian girl who understood his ambitions and thought he was quite handsome, with his spiked hair and beach tan. Remarkably, the girl had been able to handle quite a bit of liquor, so he had drunk quite a bit as well. Franko would not remember very much of the prior night and certainly not the girl's name. The police would be unable to locate this girl, and it would be called into question if she had ever existed. Unfortunately for Franko,

71

his door had somehow become propped open, so the computerized lock could not verify an alibi either. Of course, the camera on Floor 14 had chosen yesterday to stop working. It would not be fixed until at least 11:15 as Jason Conlon, the hotel repairman, would come in late. Strangely, his car simply would not start this morning. It was a terrible run of coincidences for Franko. This would leave him with no alibi and plenty of motive as Giovanni's death would lead him to rise to the top of the Montecello family. Truly unfortunate.

Before the creature shattered the mobster's femur sending him howling to the floor. Before It rained down blow after blow on his chest, smashing his splintered ribs into his lungs and heart. Before Its inhuman strength caved in the man's skull, It got close to Giovanni. It leaned in near enough to his ear that he could hear the wet separation of Its lips before It spoke.

Giovanni's trembling form felt cold breath against his ear, as It whispered an answer to his earlier inquiry.

"Tutti Frutti."

Chapter 2: Heresy

In retrospect, It should not have been surprised. The same innate abilities that had placed 34,000 in cash into his briefcase, were not at his disposal. It was not a giant asp coiling up an elevator cable in Its escape. A hundred extraneous eyes did not coat him, watching with wide eyes for an oncoming assault. At the moment, It was just a human that walked alone in a Miami alleyway at 1:24 AM.

Two ears, a range of a mere 64-23,000 hertz.
Eyes that saw rainbows with only seven colors.
And a nose meant for little more than deciding what might taste good.

More than any of that, there was something disconcerting about existing in a body that contained only a gallon of blood. The same gallon that a gallon of milk contained. This was of course something It considered far more disconcerting when two canine teeth punctured the carotid artery in Its neck.

It had forgotten vampires existed. They attended the masquerade of life together but that didn't mean they got to look beneath each other's masks. The creature tended not to concern himself with the other races of the secret world, so it was increasingly stressful for It to remember how to kill a particular type while imagining a gallon container of milk turned upside down and violently squeezed onto the floor.

There was a metal, I remember. Were they another of the ones that don't like cold iron? Or was it silver? No, wait, is that lycanthropes? Hulders? Maybe Bunyips?

The crack of an arm breaking under the vampire's

intensifying grip was the spur in Its side It needed to make a decision.

*Water. There is **some** kind of water that brings them harm. Salt water? No, river water.*

With a snap decision, Its red blood changed to cold, white, frothing, river water. The shock of a geyser spraying him in the face detached the fangs in his neck. The vampire stumbled back a few steps and bumped into the alley wall.

Damn. Bad guess.

Elder eyes gleamed red in the shadow of the alleyway. The shapeshifter knew what the creature staring back at him saw was something exotic, even to a vampire.

My skin must be a shade afield from a human's, with water running through my veins instead of blood, It thought as It touched a hand to the side of his unnaturally white neck that had been ripped open by the hunter's teeth. The spot mended with barely a thought from the creature. *His eyes grow wide like a human's. So many things seen with eyes so old, and the idea that something that can change shape into anything, would choose to favor a form without a torn neck surprises him?*

"What are you?" the vampire asked, sounding rather southern French to the shapeshifter's ears.

It blinked, and slitted eyes replaced Its previous human ones so as to be better suited for the task of watching the circling vampire in the dark. "I see quite a number of years staring back through those eyes of yours. Quite a shade they carry. A wisdom lies in a red so deep."

The vampire smiled with fangs streaked in wisdom. "Yet tonight we find them curious," came his voice, deep and dry.

Ah, now I remember, It thought, glancing at the moon in a puddle. *This will take time.*

The shapeshifter opened his mouth in a liar's smile to display knife-sharp triangular teeth that fit together like a bear trap. "There are stories."

The delicate touch of his claw-like thumbnail cut the vampire's soggy tie to the ground. "Please," he gestured with a hand full of dark potential.

I need to be careful the warping within my chest does not bump my skin, lest I give away my ruse.

To draw in red eyes, Its knuckles turned to steel and glowed red hot with slag set to drip onto the asphalt. "Some say golden dragons are so wise they may ascend beyond merely one form. Other tales, from the Norse, tell of half trolls. Mixed between natural humans and supernatural trolls, they are unbound by the realities of both, owing no shape eternity. Even Greek gods are said to change into handsome men to litter the land with bastards."

"Yes, and blues musicians sing about the devil sauntering about in different forms, tricking and trapping and all that," the vampire contributed, whilst his claws extended another half inch. "But I'm a touch too old to believe in 'god.' Elohim turned far too many tides red for me to believe he would settle down and have a kid. Give me your truth, shapeshifter."

It cracked Its neck to the left. "Truth? I am a liar. To the very core of my existence, I deceive. You're attempting to soak up the ocean in a rock. If I had a form that existed before the rest, one more *true* than the others, I could never prove it to be 'truth.' Just as you could never convince me you know the taste of anything but blood. Describe the taste of a Twinkie as more than ash. and I'll peel back this mask. You should pick a fairy tale and make that your truth."

It cracked Its neck to the right. "Else you're more likely to find yourself a pillar of salt than enlightened."

Just as some humans can juggle, there are some vampires that can do something called flitting. When vampires flit they move at speeds faster than cognition, so they use muscle memory to perform practiced, predetermined tasks. For example, one of these tasks might be to dash forward and disembowel someone. This was something the blur had done before, likely to much success. Of course, in this instance, instead of bowels the vampire found a 220-watt UV light shining back at him. The vampire staggered back with a muffled scream barely heard over the hiss of searing flesh. Stifled whimpering could be heard beneath clawed hands as smoke billowed from between his fingers.

"I spoke too soon," It amended, tearing the rest of the skin of Its torso apart with both hands. "Consider yourself enlightened."

After nearly a minute of searing the creature, the shapeshifter began to question his memory. Clearly it was effective, but this was not going to deliver a final death to this vampire. When the smoke began to lessen and a head rose, with no guise of humanity about it, the shapeshifter panicked. It went with Its first and best idea, transforming into a four-hundred-

76

pound gorilla and punching the vampire dead in the face. His head bounced off the alley wall, and he landed face first in a puddle. The shapeshifter elbow-dropped on top of him as Triple H and changed again, this time into Saint John Paul the Second. It had used the shape before and knew the man had a decent memory for Latin.

With an elderly finger, It waved a quick cross in the air and spoke with the perfect spoken Latin of Julius Caesar. "In nomine Patris, et Filii, et Spiritus San–"

The shapeshifter's words died as the vampire reached back and tore Its throat out. The pope rolled his eyes as the vampire stuck his talons through the robed man's cheek and began to rip out his jaw. The shapeshifter grew another head devoid of anything but the necessities to speak and finished the blessing. "–Sancti, Amen."

Immediately every part of the vampire making contact with the huge puddle hissed and bubbled away. The steam that spewed back at the shapeshifter reminded It of a slaughterhouse set ablaze.

This old body will hardly restrain him. Perhaps a hippo could more properly baptize him? No, elephants weigh more.

The elephant form turned out to be a mistake. It was too close to the wall and the elephant could not stay properly centered. The vampire bit his fangs through his bottom lip with exertion, but with the uneven weight, managed to flip the beast.

*Blast these forms I'm taking. I don't need the weight of an elephant. I can weigh whatever I want I can crush him beneath the weight of **me**.*

With papal fashion on the mind, It became a silver crucifix as tall as the alley was wide and fell upon Its foe. Bones cracked, and mortar sprinkled them from on high. Eyestalks, like those of a snail, grew all over the cross to watch the vampire's struggle.

The blood drinker's back is hissing too... I forgot about the church's correlation with these creatures.

Keen to capitalize on whatever Christianity had to offer, new arms robed like priests and nuns and cardinals sprouted fleshy from the metal cross with crucifixes in hand and battered the vampire's limbs and body with a meaty thump and hiss on each impact.

*I need no muscled ape when I can create my own muscles and make them as strong as I desire. I have **my** strength.*

The vampire's supporting limbs were mashed into pulp within fleshy sacks, and he splashed back down in the holy puddle. Countless bibles and candles sprouted from atop the silver cross, all sporting mouths. They spoke everything vaguely religious that John Paul II's head had in it. Prayers in Latin, prayers in English, blessings, sacraments, and of course bible verses from all over the book. Even songs and hymns were sung from pretty, ladylike lips and the lips of young, cute children. All sung to the chaotic tempo of tenderizing the vampire. To his credit, the vampire was very old and very powerful. He could heal extraordinarily fast but not fast enough to do anything with his body but have it broken and re-broken again and again.

Vampires. They form their clans and build their castles and dance clubs. They prey on humans in their dance clubs. They grow drunk on the power they hold in their silly clan politics.

*They cross their legs in throne rooms and drink priceless wine they cannot taste but a memory of. All the while they laugh at the meager existence of humans, knowing that it is **they** who go bump in the night. **They** are the scary monsters that humans make movies about. **They** go to sleep wondering if a vampire hunter will seek them out like a child does the monster in the closet. So vain are they, to imagine the shadows hold nothing that they do not know of. They occupy such a small section of the black and farther behind them in the dark **I** am there. I am always there. I **have** always been there.*

More arms grew, holding smoking censors and palms to flick holy water. Dove wings sprouted sporadically, and some flapped with a rapid panic while others sat idle with a curious ignorance to the world. Crusader swords sprouted from the bottom of the cross and passed through the vampire's flesh and the asphalt beneath with a certainty only the inanimate can express. Rosary beads wrapped around the vampire like snakes, binding him. Even the irises of Its eyestalks turned to stained glass windows as It idly observed the creature being turned to a ripple in a puddle.

He is so ancient. He's an antique, a treasure even. All of the history he must have effected. The people he must have seen... and killed. It'll all be gone in just a moment, and no one will ever really remember him. Clan members will move to fill the vacuum. Demagogues will say his name, and his underlings will breathe a breath of relief for a moment before another boot is down upon them. So grand, and all that will be left is such a pitiful remembrance.

When the only sound beneath him was that of the rosary beads cracking to dust, everything stopped. The gaping maw that was sucking in enough air to support so many voices sighed and began to melt away. All of It melted away. It turned to a writhing mass of flesh, and so that It had eyes to cry with, It became human. It would not hide from the sadness as an emotionless blob, and It didn't truly know why.

He could never have known something like me would exist in an alley in Miami. Beyond the postcard beaches, this place is like Newark with palm trees. I suppose I'm lucky they have stretches of vacancy like this. Or rather Miami is lucky it did not need to have a plague tonight.

The cross had left a cracked indentation in the pavement that the water adhered to. It was all that was left of the vampire that never even had a name to the shapeshifter. It could have become the proper machinery to repair the street, but mechanical things were sometimes a strain. And It had not had much sugar since the three king-sized candy bars on the way to the dead drop. It did not feel like over extending itself before re-fueling. That could be dangerous. At the back of Its mind was a pleasant feeling about leaving evidence that the vampire had existed. Evidence he had existed, and then stopped doing that.

I don't even know what his name was. I don't know what he did or where he came from. I'm nostalgic for some sod that might well have deserved to be wiped from this earth. So many forms, and in them all I'm so very silly.

It reached a long arm out, with enough muscle to row up a waterfall, and pulled a dumpster over to cover the spot. When It did, dread filled Its stomach. The lid was torn off in a second, and a bright anglerfish light lobe sprouting from the shapeshifter's forehead illuminated the inside of the dumpster.

The shapeshifter spoke softly, but there was something

cold about the speed at which he did. "You made a noise when your head hit the side of the box, fledgling. Pain is as temporary as immortality."

As temporary as you.

She was young. Too young to have agency anywhere for her version of eternity. The shapeshifter knew she had not been turned for *her* benefit.

He was lonely. He wanted a companion. So where there was one, he made two.

"I-I'm Clara. I'll serve you. M-my blood is your– no, wait! Your blood is the pulse that– no please I'll remember it. I can serve you. You can be my new master. You can teach me the ways of... you can show me how to be... one of..."

*She's never even fed. I was to be her first feeding. She can't even remember that silly poem they teach all the little ghouls. He should never have done this. He could have made a friend of some member of his clan. Such **narcissism** to make her just like him. No child has lived long enough to be prepared to live forever.*

"...I will make you just like me if you wish," It said slowly, to which she nodded like her un-life depended on it. "I can show you how to shapeshift right now."

She smiled a relief that was not real in any world but hers.

"Historical figures are the easiest. You like strong women, don't you? Good role models for a girl like you."

"Y-yes sire, my master, you are right!" she blurted quickly, watching Its face, now more human, looking for a reaction.

"Good... now, just think of... Joan of Arc," he said with a fingertip turning to oak. "Close your eyes and think of her short, blonde hair and gleaming armor. Focus on that gleam on her pauldron. It's reflecting the warm May sun. You are none other than France's most well known..."

The finger extended explosively like a frog's tongue and stung the girl's heart with the slightest prick.

"Hérétique," came the perfectly replicated voice of Geoffroy Thérage.

I'll remember this moment when I find myself lonely, but I could never have bound my fate to that girl. She asked too much. How could I trust her? How could I care for her? I could never have raised a child for eternity. I'm am not so lonely that I would engage in that undertaking.

The fire caught to the garbage in the dumpster, and the shapeshifter let it burn. The only light for almost a mile of city was burning trash. It illuminated his discarded briefcase, and the shapeshifter opened it. It retrieved Its smart-phone and a hundred-dollar bill.

When It walked out of that alley, Its mind was on the 7/11 store locator. Its mind was on the thirty scoops of grape Kool-Aid mix It was going to pour into a gallon jug of Hawaiian Punch. Its mind was on sour gummy worms and Fruit by the Foot. Its mind could not have been on loneliness. It could not have started wondering whether street lights and billboards were secretly his kin. It could not have begun to wonder whether It was the only one to walk around and breathe. It could not have wondered whether any of them would reveal themselves if It ran screaming what It was to everything in existence. That would have driven It mad.

Chapter 3: Research

When sugar began to be mass-produced and became much more popular, as the 1900s began to roll on, the shapeshifter had been almost frightened at what It could then do. If It really consumed the sugar It did, for the purpose of becoming a city wrecking monster, it would have been palettes of raw sugar It devoured. Of course, It had never really needed to get stronger, and the taste of raw sugar had never been terribly pleasant to the shapeshifter. Instead It sat in a cyber cafe eating religieuse, yet another creative way of packaging grotesque quantities of sugar. As the creature packed down French pastry after French pastry, It tapped the "down" key on yet another page of info on Jaeger Fleischer. It was disappointing that two thousand dollars' worth of private detective work could not definitively say it was a fake name. The shapeshifter wondered if it was a taunt. Something to show how well he could hide information.

He scratched his new beard and Alt-tabbed another window up. This one was a PDF of an arrest report. The charges were dropped because there was no tangible crime. The cops heard screams, and he was found slashing up trees. It was state land, and the locals grabbed him. Something about a forest fire and an Amber Alert made holding him an inconvenience, and they dropped his case.

Double clicking on the image file made an eyebrow go up. *A grosse messer sword? Terribly fascinated with the Germans, this one... couldn't even give him any serious weapons charge since those only **do** have one edge. They're just big knives.*

With a sigh he took off his black, thick-rimmed glasses and rubbed the bridge of his thick nose. Another Alt Tab brought up the first page he had been looking at. It was a Craig's List ad for a secretary job. Working, of course, in the office of Private Detective Jaeger Fleischer.

He checked a phone that he knew would not have any new messages or calls and took a sip of his "coffee". *Such fools to leave the syrup dispenser unattended over by the straws and sugar packets.*

No one pays secretaries forty dollars an hour unless they intend to have sex with them, or have such a high turnover rate that they need to. Another thing that caught the shapeshifter's eye was just how many things were listed before supernatural investigation and after it. Car key retrieval and teenager drug stash finding made it onto the list along with antique appraising. He reasoned that either the detective is ashamed of the fact he takes supernatural cases and hopes no one will notice, or perhaps he hopes the obfuscation will thin out the crazies. The shapeshifter thought it might have been that he would be willing to do literally anything to avoid dealing with the secret world.

It cracked Its neck to the left, and then to the right. *It's time to make my first friend.*

Chapter 4: The Interview

Craig's List did not inspire confidence. Neither did the building Detective Fleischer had chosen for his office. It was not the small apartment building one might find in an old noir flick. This had been the host of several businesses once, as it was a literal office building. In ill-fitting high-heels, she clicked passed innumerable barren cubicles and stray wheelie chairs.

The look It had gone for was the disinterested teen wearing her nagging mother's spare business attire. This allowed for disgusted sighs instead of a far more reasonable wide-eyed search for dangerous squatters or drug dealers.

The instructions given had been clear:

-Enter in the front door at 1402 Prospect Ave.
- Do NOT use the elevator. Instead, walk to the right of the reception desk.
-Take the first staircase up to the 3rd floor.
-Walk all the way down until you reach my office.
-I've turned on only the lights necessary to reach my office, so that should help.

Passing the second-floor landing, she paused. With no proper lights, it was lit red – like a horror film set in deep space – by an exit sign. She spotted a motivational poster – illuminated by the murderous hue of the second floor – that no one had wanted when their business went bankrupt. The man on it with his hands up in the air, in celebration, looked comically sarcastic under the circumstance.

The shapeshifter moved on to the third floor, where she

found a waiting room. Perhaps, *hopefully,* large for a detective office with employment ads placed on a website known for organizing orgies and drug deals. She sat down on a couch that had very likely been salvaged from some forgotten, obscure reach of the building. A relic of a long dead business.

A man of more superstition might have feared an Indiana Jones style boulder rolling after him for grabbing such an artifact.

Normally It preferred the shape of male humans, but for secretarial work it was best to adhere to stereotypes. To Its mind, both genders required an enormous amount of detail, whether they applied such detail to their persons through pampering and makeup or not. The issue with taking a female form was in the requiring of external props, such as purses and phones. These were complicated to construct and required what It considered a wasteful amount of nutrients. Instead, the shapeshifter tended towards purchasing Its own props. On the upside, it was not uncommon for women to wear or carry an item that had seen little or no use. So a newly purchased item did not particularly stand out.

The shapeshifter retrieved an iPhone with a cracked screen from miss-sized dress pants. *6:17, right on time.*

She spotted a small table without wheels and moved to drag it across the floor to use as a foot rest. Even with the muscles of a seventeen-year-old girl, she could have lifted it up to move it. Instead, it grated across the ground with a sound that could have reminded one of the screams of Gehenna.

It didn't take long for Jaeger to leave his office to find the well-crafted scene. She had popped a tooth out and turned it into bubble gum. She chewed audibly to polish it all off.

"What are you doing?" Jaeger asked, bewildered beyond the ability to articulate just how in the right he was.

"Are you ready to interview me?"

"It's six..." The detective's hand dove into a pant pocket, and scrambled for a phone. "...eighteen!"

She blew a bubble with no particular alacrity and when it popped he sprung back into being indignant.

"The meeting was a soft 5:15, not a soft..." his next words came out as gibberish through a filter of fingers. His hands slid up his face to reveal a calm expression. His hands combed his thick brown hair backwards with a sigh and a smile as false as the shapeshifter's face. "Just come on into my office and we can see about that interview."

It took him a moment to find a suitably cold Red Bull from a mini-fridge that had probably not worked since the day he'd bought it at a pawn shop going-out-of-business sale. Once he did, and sat down, it took him a moment to come up with what to say. For some people, resisting coming right out and shouting "fuck you" is difficult. But of course he couldn't, as his waiting room was not packed with alternative candidates.

"So the job is answering phones when I'm not in. Mainly that anyway. I'll also need you to conduct interviews on my behalf, sort out the crazies and stuff."

Her expression alone caused him to take a sip of his caffeine-rich beverage and consider the likelihood she might quit after a week.

"I have to deal with... *weird* people?"

"All sorts dear," the detective said behind a sympathetic smile that was probably a bit more gleeful than sympathetic. "Don't worry though, most of them don't have rabies. Now on the pay point: I will need to pay a more economical sum, than the aforementioned one, as I am paid job-to-job rather than by a consistent salary as you will be. And so it makes more sense to supply you with a salary more in tune with the business."

I'm glad he's at least a proficient liar. Good negotiator too. Bait and switch. Pay is an uncomfortable topic for most. By bringing it up himself, he's brought himself the advantage.

"That's agreeable, I hope?" he told her, more than asked, as he placed his drink down.

If I was in it for the money, I would go and assassinate someone. "Sure, whatever." She sighed with a shrug of annoyance somewhat unjustified for a teenager looking for a part-time job.

The hands of conclusion clapped together with an energy of rejection. "Great," Jaeger said, holding a smile like the sprint at the end of a marathon. "Any questions before you go?"

There were. There were quite a few that could have been asked, in fact. It could have asked to be paid per job so as to not tax the business unduly. It could have asked if he would work with something like It. It could have asked if he had ever seen anything like It. It could have asked him to give It a name. It could have asked him to be Its friend.

"No... I'm good"

And the shapeshifter was. After all this *was* a good start.

There Are No White Knights

Malric did not believe himself a good man. He had burned no villages, nor raped any women. But to go down the list of evil he had *not* done would not paint him well, for it was not quite long enough to be proud of. What evils he had not done were not due to his inner sense of justice or overpowering will to bring light upon the land. He had not committed a great many wicked tasks because he happened not to be ordered to. That did not make him a good man; it made him a knight.

Three and a half minutes placed him here, in this armor, with arena gravel beneath his feet. Knights were problems solved. They swore loyalty and to never seek power. Real power, over estates and land, was for elder brothers. Malric would never be like his brother, pretending that he could be a good man. Maelenn's power would always take away his own choices like it took away Malric's. The job of a governor is never actually governing. It is to play the game of politics.

Malric would fight today in the tournament because it would help his brother play that game. It was the princess's marriage celebration, and all the knights of the realm would be coming to show their worth.

In between rich people fighting, however, were peasants. Dressed up like fools at court in borrowed armor and swinging borrowed weapons. They were provided these things and the coin incentive to win. This secondary bracket of peasantry provided the excitement of death missing in a contest of nobles.

For anyone to kill a noble would mean death. A highborn gets the axe, while peasants are disemboweled and pulled apart by horses. Hollow stares from atop the city walls remind all within what peasants are. Food for crows.

As Malric watched, he knew one of these peasants would die. They were not afforded the same safety that nobles held.

"Who d'ya think will win this one? Sir." Asked the rosy-cheeked lad fastening Malric's gauntlet.

The knight squinted at the fighters in question. "You use a blade curved forward to hack better, backward to cut, and a straight sword is balanced and can thrust efficiently. Blondie has two and both will not pierce his opponent's chainmail. Not unless he manages to stab with those curved things of his."

"But ain't the other man just as flogged?" the squire asked, as he rummaged through a chest of armor.

"Well, he's chosen poorly. He's got a hammer, but blunt weapons are more for platemail than anything, and his opponent has leather. Not that a sturdy piece of steel won't break a skull, but one crack on a fully armored knight, and his enemy would have his ears ringing so bad his helm would be full of vomit."

Platemail was hard and smooth, so blades did little but glance off. If you wanted to kill a man in plate, you were better off holding the sword by the blade and clubbing him with the crossguard. The shape of the armor did nothing to defend against blunt weapons.

"Twenty laurels on the ratty one," came a soft rasp beside him.

Malric spared a glace to see Sir Caleb. Still not in his armor. "Prince Caleb."

He loved that. "What a laugh you are! I'm not a prince. I've not married the princess nearly yet."

No. You have not.

Caleb had a pointed nose and a jaw that could cut timber. His hair was black and forever bound back in his signature tight ponytail. He was far more attractive than Malric.

Caleb gave a playful rap on Malric's vambrace. A pat on the shoulder would have looked awkward as it would have been a bit of a reach. The bald man was seven foot *without* armor. He was far larger than Caleb.

"Ah!" Caleb exclaimed, as a crimson spray marked someone's end. "You should have taken that bet, friend. Looks like you would have been twenty laurels richer."

Friend? I am no friend of his.

"I'll see you on the field. I've got to be off to dedicate this match to my love."

Their union often kept the large knight awake past when a

93

man should succumb to dream. This was not rooted in any affection for the girl. He did not like them young like Caleb did. Malric remembered the night Caleb's sister killed herself. He saw Caleb leave her chambers that night, drunk enough not to remember what he had said to Malric by the morning. She left her room soon after her brother, with blood staining the front of her nightgown and dead eyes that looked past Malric towards the rampart. He didn't stop her, nor did he ask her why. It was not a knight's place to question or make demands of a noble's daughter.

"Sir?"

His armor clinked as he shifted to face the squire. "What, boy?"

"Will you be taking your Longsword again?" the child repeated.

*This time I will **know** I made the right decision.*

"Yes," he said, exhaling. "And one more thing. Strap my flanged mace to my back and put the plain tower shield, over it, on my back."

The squire's eyes opened wide. "But... **Sir–**"

Malric handed the kid a bag, from his belt, so heavy the squire had to hold it with two hands. "Tell your mother those cookies were excellent. Perhaps she could open a bakery one day."

The boy's mouth hung open when he peeked inside the bag. "But you can't–"

"And the gripping chalk, tied on the left of my belt. Now, boy. I do not pay you to gawk."

The boy did not question his better again. He strapped what he could to the knight from tip-toes atop his step ladder. As always, he needed to just hand the giant his helm.

Malric fastened his beaked helm into place and took the blade from his squire before making his way to the center of the arena. His opponent had been busy handing a white rose to an uncomfortable princess, so he was not dressed for battle. Malric rested his hands on the pommel of his sword and pressed the tip into the ground.

*He's like a child. Making the whole world wait for him to put his armor on. Making the **king** wait.*

Malric watched as Caleb donned his dark gray armor. On the chest guard was a top-down view of his own family crest: a white rose. It made for a good contrast on his dark armor. The entire suit was aesthetically pleasing, from the long white helmet comb to the spiked sabatons.

Malric's own armor was a stark contrast. His was screaming memory of the blades that had sparked together before it. He washed away blood as a courtesy to others. The knight would always know how many had died screaming at the edge of his sword. Each scratch was the desperate stroke of a dead man. Malric had, without fail, killed all who had ever struck him in battle. Each nick and dent was another gallon of blood that fed the grass.

Caleb too chose a longsword but, of course, he was not quite tall enough to backdraw the weapon, unlike Malric. His squire held out the scabbard and Caleb dragged the weapon along as he walked toward the center of the arena. The man let the tip of a sword, more expensive than the yearly pay of ten castle maids, scrape along behind him. As Malric watched, he knew this fight would not be an easy one. It was bad men who were good at killing. Men like Caleb took joy in slaughter and like a great artist puts passion into every stroke of his brush, so did he in the strokes of his sword.

With a grin burrowed in his helm, Caleb pointed his sword at Malric with one hand, and Malric mirrored him. They brought their blades vertically across their faces, then finished the salute whipping their swords down diagonally to their rights. When they did so, trumpets sounded the beginning of their match.

They both attacked each other with fervor. Sparks caught every other block. Neither made a single footing mistake without doing it to lay a trap. Longswords move fast, and so did their fight. It was not long before Malric thrust at Caleb while back pedaling. Caleb took the bait and batted it away, only to find his blade was met with about as much resistance as a waterfall. This dropped the tip of his sword to the ground. As Caleb's edge was skating off the sword, Malric brought his blade around to lay across his opponent's shoulder. Malric needed only take two steps forward, one of which was on top of Caleb's sword, knocking it from his grip. Malric's weapon scraped against the white rose knight's helm, making it clear that if they had been fighting to the death, it would have cut deep enough into Caleb's neck to end him.

In the eternity of a second, they stood face to face. Malric saw fury in Caleb's eyes. He saw a smile too, but eyes told more truth. In another heartbeat a victory trumpet sounded the end of the first round. They backed away from each other and reset for a new round.

I'm better, and now we both know.

Caleb's squire came sprinting over to pick up his sword and present it, out of breath, before jogging away. Not once did Caleb glance away from Malric as he accepted it.

As soon as the new round started, Malric adopted a blatant defensive stance with both hands gripping his sword above his head as though preparing to strike down with all his might. It was such an obvious trap that Malric hoped it might insult the already angry Caleb. If Caleb charged now, he would have him.

Malric heard him scoff. "You really think–"

*Well then, lets try **this**.*

Like a madman, Malric flung his sword one-handed at the white rose knight. It landed pommel-first into Caleb's face mask with an explosion of laughter from the crowd. With his other hand he pulled free his shield and charged Caleb, ramming him full force with all his weight just as he drew his flanged mace, swung it over Caleb, and switched back to strike him in the back. A headbutt for good measure ensured Caleb would be knocked prone.

The crowd grew silent. This was not a match now.

One kick, and the sword was out of Caleb's reach. Like a volley of arrows, Malric rained down blows. He hammered until neither arm would save Caleb. A knight was like a turtle. Laden with so much armor, Caleb could not stand without assistance. That was what squires were for.

97

Malric tossed away his shield and grabbed at the pouch of gripping chalk at his side. He slapped a handful over his chest with a puff and smeared the white powder until the hawk of his family crest was covered.

*No one but **I** will hold responsibility for this.*

Malric hastily unbuckled his enemy's helm and tossed it away. Beneath was a furious Caleb, too stunned and winded to curse him.

One strike to the center of his chest made a bang and quickened the flailing of Caleb's legs. The second made a crunch and stopped them.

Malric discarded the mace and retrieved his sword. They were coming to stop him now. He had to hurry.

"**What**!?" Caleb spat dryly between bloodied teeth. "Are you some white knight now?!"

"I'm no hero," Malric laughed, out of breath, as he set his sword to the crater he had made in Caleb's breast plate. "But I will say," he puffed with a smile, "today, I slay a ***dragon***."

Malric's gauntlets twisted tightly over the leather wrap of the sword's grip.

Malric raised the hilt above his head with both hands. "And today I'll save the ***princess***."

Acknowledgments

I suppose I should start by thanking you, whoever you are, for reading this book. Beyond that I think I should thank everyone who took the time to read over my stories and give me feedback over the years. Chief among them my good friend Maya who gave me a comprehensive edit of all of my stories and provided me with extremely useful feedback all for the promise of some gluten free cookies. I want to also thank my friend Brian for rounding out my fantasy slash grammar knowledge and giving a couple of these stories a good look. I should also thank my *brother* Brian for his non-grammar based *feelings* on what sounds right, as well as letting me know what is confusing to someone with exceptionally poor reading comprehension, as well as being my 24/7 "what do you think of this line?" consultant, **and** designing my amazing website. Seriously, thank you. I also want to thank my oldest and closest friend Conor for all his opinions on my different stories he has provided me which I consider with a great deal of weight, as well as the rare but precious words of wisdom. Like that advice about writing for the people who hang on each sentence instead of the people who skim paragraphs? You know the one. Thank you. And thank you for working your graphics magic to make the cover exist and not just be a pretty picture. And thank you Jorge Jacinto of JJcanvas for the extraordinarily pretty picture on the cover. Speaking of pretty I should thank my buddy Tait for letting me base a line or two on his own words.

Of course I should thank my parents for their years of support, finding me workshops and, of course, making me exist and all that. On that matter I should thank anyone who has ever given me words of encouragement or wished me well on my path.

I've learned a lot about writing from a lot of places but I think I should take a moment to say thank you to Hirsh Sawhney, a professor that rose above the sea of easy going workshop professors who hand out A's and personalized false hope like they're outside a metal concert giving away bibles. I expected college to be a place where I would be constantly challenged and bombarded with useful mind-blowing concepts that would change how I write and Professor Hirsh's class was the first to live up to those expectations. If I could load up 21 credits of getting my ass kicked like that every semester I would. And thank you for your words of personal support as well.

Last but most certainly not least I want to thank my trumpet teacher turned guitar teacher turned writing sensei, Rob Henke. Without Rob I would never have been inspired to start writing. Rob taught me more than anyone has about writing. I learned the basics. I learned how to edit my own work and keep my sentences concise. Most importantly he got me to understand the importance of punctuation and grammar at an age where I wasn't totally behind the whole period thing. I learned different punctuation mark could shape how a reader would read a sentence and at that time it was mind-blowing. So thank you.

Also to anyone who likes this book and tells a friend or writes a review: Thank you, sincerely. It really helps me out. If you haven't done either of those things and you did in fact like this book then you can go ahead and feel free to do those things and then come back and read the first line of this paragraph and I'll be talking to you.

www.ingramcontent.com/pod-product-compliance
Lightning Source LLC
Chambersburg PA
CBHW020729250626
47155CB00006B/2220